"Ben!"

The shock or fear or sor
voice had him rushing a
find her. She stood only a few feet from the back of the cabin in a small clearing that was overgrown with grass and weeds but it was the three wooden crosses that had him stalling in his tracks.

Moving on autopilot, Ben stamped through the knee-high grass until he reached the crosses. Three in a neat row. No markings or names. Just three rustic crosses.

Ben went down on his knees and pressed his hands to the ground. He felt the surface, touched the wood where it had been driven in the ground.

Could his father and the others be here?

Could they have been here all along?

WHISPERING WINDS WIDOWS

USA TODAY Bestselling Author

DEBRA WEBB

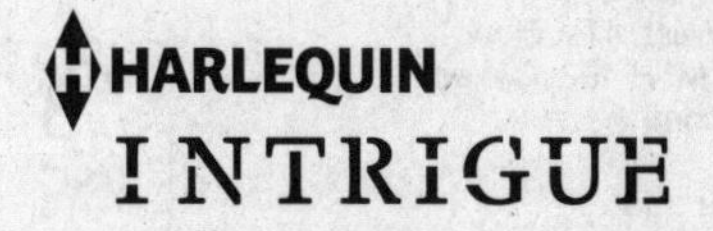

Recycling programs for this product may not exist in your area.

ISBN-13: 978-1-335-59151-7

Whispering Winds Widows

For questions and comments about the quality of this book, please contact us at CustomerService@Harlequin.com.

Harlequin Enterprises ULC
22 Adelaide St. West, 41st Floor
Toronto, Ontario M5H 4E3, Canada
www.Harlequin.com

Printed in Lithuania

Debra Webb is the award-winning *USA TODAY* bestselling author of more than one hundred novels, including those in reader-favorite series Faces of Evil, the Colby Agency and Shades of Death. With more than four million books sold in numerous languages and countries, Debra has a love of storytelling that goes back to her childhood on a farm in Alabama. Visit Debra at debrawebb.com.

Books by Debra Webb

Harlequin Intrigue

Lookout Mountain Mysteries

Disappearance in Dread Hollow
Murder at Sunset Rock
A Place to Hide
Whispering Winds Widows

A Winchester, Tennessee Thriller

In Self Defense
The Dark Woods
The Stranger Next Door
The Safest Lies
Witness Protection Widow
Before He Vanished
The Bone Room

Colby Agency: Sexi-ER

Finding the Edge
Sin and Bone
Body of Evidence

Faces of Evil

Dark Whispers
Still Waters

Visit the Author Profile page at Harlequin.com.

CAST OF CHARACTERS

Reyna Hart—Reyna writes the stories of people who are suffering from illnesses that steal their memories. The stories allow them to hold on to their pasts.

Ben Kane—Thirty years ago, his father and his two best friends disappeared without a trace. Ben would do anything to solve that mystery, more for his beloved grandfather than for himself.

The Widows—Lucinda Kane, Deidre Fuller and Harlowe Evans have secrets they can never tell. Did they murder their husbands? How far will they go to keep their secrets?

Father Vincent Cullen—He knows the truth but his vows prevent him from telling another living soul...but there are other things he can do. How far will he go to see that the secrets are revealed?

Deputy Gordon Walls—He was supposed to marry Lucinda, until she cheated on him and married someone else. Was it revenge for that betrayal that caused three men to vanish thirty years ago?

Wade Landon—He was the most succesful high school football coach in state history, but he has secrets too...secrets he can never tell anyone.

Sheriff Tara Norwood—Her father was the sheriff thirty years ago when three men disappeared. She feels obligated to finish that case for him.

Chapter One

The Light Memory Care Center
Lantern Pointe
Chattanooga, Tennessee
Sunday, April 21, 10:00 a.m.

"Are you certain you want to do this, Reyna?"

Reyna Hart smiled—as much to reassure her friend as to brace herself. She was going to do this. "I absolutely do want to do this."

Eudora Davenport's eyes shone with excitement. "I knew you'd never be able to resist." She placed a frail hand against her chest. "You don't know how much this means to me."

Reyna had a fairly good idea. She had been visiting Eudora, a sweet woman she'd enjoyed getting to know, for nearly a year now. Each Sunday from 10:00 until 11:00 a.m., sometimes until noon. Generally, they sat in the two chairs positioned to take in the view out the one large window in her room. Their tea on the table between them. They had become friends. Good friends.

"There aren't many who will talk to you," Eudora reminded her. "Others will say plenty just to hear themselves talk." She drew in a deep breath. "Some will attempt to mislead you. Folks don't always tolerate change very well. Particularly if that change prompts the unknown."

"I'm aware." Reyna considered herself a good judge of character. When she'd been pursuing her original career dream, she'd spent most of her research time interviewing people—and Eudora was right. The best interviewers learned to recognize the difference between a thoughtful and forthright person and a conversational narcissist. Reyna had spent most of her life, even as a child, watching people. Her mother always said that particular skill was one of the things that made Reyna so perfect for the art of storytelling. She was a natural at slipping into the thoughts and dreams of characters.

Reyna had certainly expected she would spend her life writing fiction. She'd been writing short stories since she'd been old enough to string sentences together. The first contract had come quickly and somewhat easier than she'd anticipated. Her debut novel had made a brief and distant showing on the bestseller lists. Not so shabby. But that book had been the one and only.

Just call her a one-semi-hit wonder.

The marketable ideas had stopped coming, and her publisher had moved on.

For a while Reyna had drifted—career wise. She'd held on to her New York City apartment that was about the size of a shoebox for another year, and then she'd opted to take a break from the dream and spend some time in reality.

Not so much fun at first. Coming back to Chattanooga to start over hadn't been easy. She'd tried out a few different career hats—none worth remembering. And though the process had been painful, the timing had turned out to be important: her beloved grandmother had been diagnosed with Alzheimer's. From that moment there had been no looking back for Reyna. She'd become her grandmother's primary caretaker even after she'd had to move to this very facility. Throughout the remainder of her life, her grandmother's greatest fear had not been of dying but of forgetting who she was and what her life had been before, so she'd asked Reyna to write her story. Then, anytime she wished, she could read her story and remember.

Reyna would have done anything for her grandmother, so she'd thrown herself into the task. The story, mostly a narrative written in first person, had given her grandmother much pleasure the final months of her life. When she'd passed, others at the facility had pleaded with Reyna to write theirs. So, she'd decided to give the possibility a go.

Now, two years later, work was steady and surprisingly lucrative. Reyna had been featured in the *Chattanooga Times Free Press*, and several other newspapers had carried her work in their lifestyle sections. She'd even received an award from the city for innovation in supporting quality of life for the elderly.

"You've decided how to start?" Eudora asked, drawing Reyna out of the past.

"I have." She gave her friend a nod. "I'm starting with Ward Kane Senior."

Eudora's thin gray brows rose. "He may not talk to you. At the ten-year anniversary of the disappearance as well as the twenty, he refused to give an interview. He's a stubborn man."

Reyna had heard this from her before. "He's also the only remaining father."

Eudora's gaze turned distant. "Sometimes I forget how much time has really gone by." She sighed. "Thirty years. It's hard to believe."

Eudora Davenport remained a beautiful woman even at eighty-two. Her hair was that perfect shade of silver that required no dyes or anything at all to give it luster or to add thickness. She wore it in a French twist with pearl pins. At this stage she spent much of her time reclined in her bed or in her favorite chair, but her loungewear was always tasteful and representative of her elegance and class. Eudora insisted aging was a gift, one that should be respected and embraced with dignity.

"I will call him," she said then, her tone determined. "Perhaps I can persuade him."

"It couldn't hurt," Reyna agreed. "I've read everything about the case that has been released for public consumption. Anything he hasn't shared could prove helpful. The FBI agent who assisted the sheriff's office in the investigation has passed away, but the deputy detective, Nelson Owens, who worked the case, has agreed to meet with me tomorrow."

Eudora picked up her cup of tea from the table between them and sipped. When she'd set it aside once more, she searched Reyna's face for a long moment before speaking. Reyna hadn't quite decided why this case was so important to Eudora. She was not related to one or more of the three men—the Three, as they were called—who had disappeared, nor the wives and children—if any—they had left behind.

The only thing she had told Reyna when she'd commissioned her to write the story that was technically not even hers was that she wanted to know the truth before she lost herself completely or died—whichever came first.

Eudora stared straight ahead for a long moment, her gaze reaching somewhere beyond the window. There were times like this when she stopped speaking and drifted off. Sometimes for minutes, others for hours. Her grandmother had done the same. Reyna had learned to be patient or to come back another time.

"She never comes to see me anymore," Eudora said, her voice as distant as her gaze.

"Who?" Reyna asked, though she wasn't sure the eighty-two-year-old was speaking to her or if she was still aware Reyna was in the room. It happened more and more lately.

Her pulse reacted to a prick of emotion. She truly had begun to consider this woman family. There was little left of Reyna's. She still had her mother, who had remarried recently and was quite focused on her new husband. Not that Reyna resented this one little bit. Her mother had been madly in love with Reyna's father, and his death had devastated them both. It had taken a decade and a half for her mother to even consider having dinner with a romantic interest. Now she was happily married to the second love of her life, and Reyna was incredibly grateful for her second chance.

Reyna, however, was still waiting for her first chance. But she had time. Thirty-five wasn't so old.

Wasn't so young either, an evil little voice chided.

"Eudora, who do you mean?" Reyna prodded.

Eudora blinked, turned away from the window to meet Reyna's gaze. "I'm sorry—what were you saying?"

"You said she never comes to see you anymore."

A frown lined the older woman's otherwise perfectly smooth brow. The woman had beautiful skin with so few lines one would think she'd had multiple cosmetic surgeries, but when asked, Eudora always laughed and insisted it was simply good genes. "Just an old friend. No one important, dear."

"Well." Reyna stood, walked over to her chair, reached for her hand and gave it a little squeeze. "I should be on my way. I can check in at the bed-and-breakfast after lunch. I'll spend some time getting the lay of the land, so to speak."

Eudora held on to her hand when Reyna would have pulled it away. "No matter what happens, I so thoroughly appreciate that you have agreed to do this for me. Please know that if you don't find the answer quickly enough or at all, don't despair. Knowing what happened is important to me, but it is not your fault if I go first."

Reyna smiled and gave her hand another squeeze. "I'm sure you'll be fine, and if I can uncover the truth, I will revel in writing the story."

Eudora released Reyna's hand and clasped hers together in her lap. "Oh, I have no doubt you'll find the truth. From the moment I met you, I was certain you would know exactly how to do what no one else could."

No pressure.

"I'll talk to you soon," Reyna promised before leaving.

This lady had a great deal of faith in her. She surely hoped she wouldn't have to let her down. A thirty-year-old missing persons case that no one else had been able to solve was a tall order.

In time, evidence grew faint, disappeared, as did memories. But there was a flip side. The passage of vast amounts of time often loosened tongues and added to the weight of guilt. Reyna exited the facility and drew in a deep breath of cool spring air. So much had started to bloom already—it gave her hope that anything could happen.

Even solving a very, very cold case.

Whispering Winds
1:00 p.m.

LEGEND HAD IT that the air in Whispering Winds was never still. The small community was an old one, nestled against the state line, nearly in Georgia. The tourist guides called it one of Lookout Mountain's lesser-known gems. Like most of the small niche communities on the mountain, the tiny town proved a powerful draw for tourists with its incredible views and ghost stories that were nearly legend in themselves. Not the least of which was the story of how three young men—Ward Kane Junior, known as JR, Duke Fuller and Judson Evans, ranging in age from twenty-eight to twenty-nine, all three with wives, one with a child—had just vanished into thin air, never to be seen again.

Reyna turned into the small parking area of the lovely historic home that had been turned into the Jewel, a bed-and-breakfast located right as you entered Whispering Winds. The house was the first of many grand old residences that had been well maintained and remained occupied. A bit farther down Main Street the town shops and offices lined both sides. Tourism kept the little shops thriving. Many of the residents worked in Chattanooga, but there were a good number of retail and service jobs available locally.

The sheer number of thriving little communities on the mountain had surprised Reyna. There was Dread Hollow and Sunset Cove, and both had their own tourist draws. Funny, when Reyna had returned to Tennessee she'd expected to end up in Nashville after spending some time with her grandmother, but fate had seen things differently.

Now she owned her grandmother's cottage in the city's historic district. Growing up, Reyna had found the little cottage filled with hidden treasures and treats. Since Reyna was the only grandchild, her grandmother had loved creating little treasure hunts and mysteries to solve whenever she'd visited. As a child, Reyna had been convinced her grandmother had secret fairy friends. She was also certain she had inherited her creativity from her dear grandmother.

The city wasn't so far, and Reyna could have opted to drive back and forth for the next few days while she did this deep dive into research, but in her experience, there was no substitute for living among the folks from whom she wanted answers.

Reyna parked her vintage Land Rover—also inherited from her grandmother—in a spot reserved for guests and climbed out. Owning a vehicle in New York City had been far too much trouble. The better route had been just to rent one when needed. But here, in the South, a vehicle was a must. Reyna had always loved the Land Rover, and her grandmother had insisted she take possession of it as soon as she moved back home. Even for a vehicle nearing forty years old, it had very low mileage and was in pristine condition, aesthetically and mechanically.

She grabbed her bag from the back seat and headed up the walk. Spring flowers were blooming, and the trees had sprouted new leaves. The world was coming alive, her grandmother would say, after its long winter's sleep.

The porch was exactly what one expected of a grand Victorian home. It spread across the front and wrapped around one side. More than a century old, the home stood three floors high and covered better than thirteen thousand square feet. Lots of stone taken right from the area made up the foundation and the walkways. But it was the fountains and gardens that took her breath away before she even reached the entrance. Truly beautiful. So well-thought-out.

Stepping inside, Reyna found exactly what she'd anticipated. Soaring ceilings and grand chandeliers. Furniture made during a time when craftsmanship had carried a higher standard. Shiny wood floors and well-loved woven rugs.

The registration desk was staffed by the owner. Reyna recognized Birdie Jewel from the website's About page. A lovely woman of somewhere in her late seventies, with the gray hair to prove it. Her hair hung in a long, loose braid. She looked up and smiled, and her eyes were bright in a face that showed a light hand toward cosmetics. As natural as Birdie Jewel's gray hair and minimal makeup suggested she might be, her style in clothing was the show. Flamboyant fabrics in brilliant colors. Lots of exotic jewelry that tinkled as she moved around the counter to meet Reyna.

"Welcome. You must be Reyna Hart."

Her voice was as musical as her jewelry. Pleasantly so.

"Hello." Reyna dropped her bag at her feet and shook the woman's outstretched hand. "This is genuinely lovely." She gazed around the lobby.

Birdie's smile widened. "Oh, I adore hearing guests say so. Come sign the guest book." She hurried behind the counter once more and turned the large guest book around to face Reyna. "We do things here a little on the old-fashioned side. None of your personal information will be in the book, but we do love for you to sign your name. Even if only your given name."

"Love that." Reyna accepted the pen and signed her name on the next available line. She passed the pen back to the owner.

"Now I'll need your credit card."

"Of course."

Once the paperwork was done, Birdie grabbed a key from one of the numbered boxes behind the desk. "Follow me," she said.

Reyna picked up her bag and trailed after Birdie, who

led the way up the grand staircase, her bohemian skirt flowing around her. It wasn't until they neared the top that Reyna noticed the older woman was barefoot. Her toenails were painted a bright orange. Reyna smiled. She preferred bare feet herself when working at home.

The owner paused in front of room seven. "This one is for you. It has the balcony that overlooks Main Street."

"Lovely." Some might prefer one of the views provided from the elegant home's cliff-side location, but she was interested in what was happening among the people, so a view of Main Street was perfect.

"Make yourself at home," Birdie said as she placed the key on the table near the door. "If you need anything at all, just let me know. I'm always here. Breakfast is served each morning from seven until nine. Snacks are always available, but we serve no other organized meals."

"Perfect," Reyna assured her.

When the lady had gone, after closing the door behind her, Reyna quickly hung up the clothes she had brought along. She put away her suitcase and left her toiletry bag in the bathroom. The claw-foot tub was center stage in the room. Very romantic.

Reyna walked out onto the balcony and simply stood there for a long while. She watched the slow pace of the cars moving along Main Street and the even slower stride of the pedestrians. The small town had a very sedate air about it. Peaceful, content. And yet thirty years ago the Three had disappeared without a trace.

The wives left behind remained, to this day, widowed. For thirty years all three had stuck with their stories of having no idea what had become of their husbands. Never a single deviation, not even a little one. Those closest to the families had given mixed messages, according to the many, many articles Reyna had read. Most were certain the couples had all been happily married. Churchgoing, deeply in love, happy people with no financial issues or other known troubles.

The men had been lifelong best friends. Different jobs, different family backgrounds. As adults they'd remained friends, and the women they'd married, Lucinda, Deidre and Harlowe, had been best friends their entire lives as well. They'd attended school together, parties, vacations, and they'd all married the same summer—only days between their weddings.

So strange that the men would abruptly disappear together and the women would know nothing of the reason. Not one had ever remarried. Not one had ever spoken against the other.

Reyna walked back into her room, closed the French doors to the balcony and decided she would drive around a bit and get the lay of the land.

Tonight she would call Eudora and tell her all that she'd seen. The woman couldn't wait to hear everything.

Eudora was such a good storyteller in her own right that developing her narrative would be incredibly easy. Reyna had videoed their sessions using her phone's camera, as she did with all clients, and then she would use those to help bring their voices to life.

The sun was shining and the temperature was perfect for a leisurely stroll, but Reyna wanted to drive to a number of locations first thing, so she opted to head out to the Land Rover. She'd grab some lunch somewhere before returning to the Jewel.

Excitement had her belly tingling as she descended the staircase. To tell the truth, she hadn't felt this much enthusiasm for an endeavor since her own book. She enjoyed all her work, but this was the first time she had felt so drawn toward a project. She wanted to find the answers that no one else had. When she'd written her novel, a mystery loosely based on an actual event, she had loved the research aspect. The digging into the dirty details in search of previously unearthed facts.

Perhaps that was what had put the fire in her blood this time. Her goal was to find the answer to a thirty-year-old mystery. Had the young husbands taken off for parts unknown in search of wealth or new love? Had they met with untimely deaths from someone to whom they had been in some sort of debt?

Or were the Widows actually murderers who had decided for whatever reasons that their husbands had to die?

The Widows of Whispering Winds. The perfect book or movie title. For the first five or so years after the disappearance of the Three—no remains had ever been found—there had been lots written on the Widows and the long-lost husbands. But the story had eventually fizzled as they all did. Once in a great while a retired cop or private investigator or investigative reporter would come to town and dig around. But no one had ever found an answer.

Reyna refused to allow that reality to dampen her spirit. In all such unsolved cases, there were no answers until someone found one. It was only a matter of time and interest. And maybe luck.

She had the time and the interest. Just maybe she would get lucky.

The idea that this could be more than the memoir for Eudora dared to flirt with her thoughts. This could be Reyna's next book.

Eudora herself had suggested as much.

"Don't get ahead of yourself, girl."

Reyna started her Land Rover and prepared to back out of the parking lot. A knot tightened in her stomach. She wasn't getting her hopes up about anything more than what was. She would write the memoir and dig as deep into this mystery as necessary to find answers for her client.

Nothing more…for now.

If more developed…well, that would be incredible. For now, all her focus needed to be on finding answers.

The knot loosened, and Reyna eased the Land Rover out onto Main Street. She surveyed the lovely shops and the happy-looking pedestrians. It was all picture-perfect. Like a Norman Rockwell painting. The quintessential little village filled with the best of what life had to offer.

But there was something unpleasant or perhaps evil hidden here.

All Reyna had to do was find it.

Chapter Two

Kane Residence
Lula Lake Lane
3:30 p.m.

"Ben, I think that faucet in the bathroom under the stairs is dripping a little too."

Bennett "Ben" Kane drew his upper body from under the kitchen sink and looked over at his grandfather. "I'm just about finished under here, so I'll have a look at that one next."

He swiped his hand over the interior floor of the sink base cabinet to ensure no water had dripped from the P-trap he'd replaced. Dry as a bone. Good to go. He grabbed his tools, elbowed the cabinet doors shut and got to his feet.

"That's a wrap on this one. Good thing too. The old one was just about rusted through."

Ward Kane Senior, arms crossed over his chest, gave an approving nod from where he was propped against the counter overseeing the work. "A man can't complain when anything lasts fifty years."

Ben placed the wrenches in his toolbox. "No, sir, he sure can't."

His grandfather's father had built this house. Fifty

years ago his grandfather had renovated this kitchen after inheriting the place. Ben's own daddy had been born in this house. There was a lot of Kane history here. It was home.

For the past year, Ben had been living here...*again.*

"I'll make a pot of coffee." Ward Senior moved toward the sink, his gait unsteady still.

The hip-replacement surgery had gone well but, as the old man would say, nothing had worked the same since. His hand shook when he reached for the carafe. A frown tugged at Ben's brow. The shaking hands was different. He'd keep a closer watch for any worsening. His grandfather would be the first to say that at eighty-five things started to wear out, but Ben felt it was his obligation to keep a running list of anything the doctor might need to hear about. Otherwise, the good doctor would likely never know.

"I'll be right with you," Ben promised. He grabbed his toolbox from the counter and headed for the bathroom beneath the stairs, which was more a powder room with just a toilet and sink.

He tapped the newel-post as he passed it, as was his habit. He'd spent a lot of time on those bottom three steps as a kid. He could sit there and watch through the glass in the front door for his daddy to come pick him up. Not that Ben hadn't enjoyed spending time with his grandparents—he had. But his father had worked long hours in the city. Sometimes late into the evenings. So on the occasional Saturdays or Sundays when his parents had left him with his grandparents, he'd always been anxious to get home. He'd loved his daddy and hadn't had nearly enough time with him.

Ben pushed the memories aside. No point going there

today. Today was for his grandfather—his pops, as he had fondly referred to him since he'd been old enough to talk. There were things around the house that needed a little tweaking, and until now, his grandfather had refused to allow Ben to take care of them. He'd insisted that as soon as he was recovered from his surgery he'd intended to do it himself. Here they were nearly a year later, and finally he'd relented and agreed to have the work done.

Ben placed his toolbox on the toilet lid and studied the fifty-odd-year-old sink faucet. Sure enough, about every five seconds a drop of water slipped free. His grandfather's eighty-five-year-old body might've been giving out here and there, but the man's hearing was perfect. Lying in bed at night, he probably heard every drop hit that porcelain sink basin. Ben chuckled.

Ward Kane Senior had spent his whole life from age twelve until just last year as the local handyman in Whispering Winds. He'd been taking care of folks' around-the-house issues for all that time. His son, Ward Junior, had started helping him when he'd been twelve as well. But then when he'd married, his wife—Ben's mom—had insisted that she wasn't living that life. She'd wanted a husband with a "real job that paid real money." So his father had gone to work for a plumbing company down in Chattanooga, and Ben wasn't sure his grandfather had forgiven his mother yet.

Ben was fairly confident the two would never do more than merely tolerate each other and would only do that because of him.

Some family rifts just couldn't be repaired. Maybe if his father had still been with them things would have turned out differently.

"Enough of that," he grumbled as he focused on changing the washer in the faucet.

The truth was Ben hadn't done the right thing either. His mother had insisted that he go to college, so he had. He'd spent the past twelve-plus years as an architect in Chattanooga, helping out his grandfather here and there. But last year, with his grandfather's health declining and his longtime helper having moved away, Ben had had to move in for a while.

The wrench slipped, and he popped his knuckles on the sink rim. He swore under his breath.

Well, he could have driven in from the city and then back home at night, but his two-year relationship with the woman he'd expected to marry had ended, and he'd decided that going home no longer held much appeal. Not that he could blame his ex-fiancée so much. The trouble had been more his fault than hers. He'd been so focused on work that he'd allowed their relationship to disintegrate. It would be far easier to blame her for finding someone new, but then, it might not have happened if he had been paying attention.

He wasn't sure they had ever decided what they'd wanted for the future. They'd never talked about starting a family or any aspect of long term. Once they'd been engaged, things had just sort of stalled there. In hindsight they'd probably rushed into the engagement thing too quickly anyway. Better to move on before things got any more complicated.

No hard feelings was always the best way if it was doable.

At some point he would likely put his house in the city on the market. He was perfectly happy here for now. His mother, on the other hand, was not happy at all. She wanted him back in the city and getting on with his life. Not going backward, as she called it.

"Coffee's done!" his grandfather shouted.

Ben smiled. Coffee with his grandfather on a Sunday afternoon was always a good thing.

Ben finished up, grabbed his toolbox and headed back to the kitchen. "Next week I need to get up on this roof," he said as he left his tools on the bench by the back door. "Those April showers have given me a pretty good idea where the leaks are."

There were only two and those only showed up during a serious downpour, but they needed to be taken care of before they worsened.

"No need." Ward filled his cup and settled at the table. "I called Johnson's Roofing. I'm just gonna have the whole thing replaced with one of those nice metal ones. They have a special right now. Ten percent discount."

Ben blew out a long, low whistle as he filled his own cup. "Standing seam metal roof—that'll be a pretty penny, Pops."

"I've got plenty of pretty pennies," he said with a pointed look in Ben's direction. "Planning to get the place painted too."

Now Ben was worried. "You planning on selling? Or are you just trying to make me feel unneeded?"

"The place hasn't been painted in thirty years," Ward declared. He gingerly sipped his steaming brew.

"I thought you liked the chippy-white-paint style." Ben grinned at the hard look cast his way. "You know, I'm a pretty good painter."

"You've got enough on your hands with taking care of folks in the community and still doing projects for that firm of yours."

"Technically," Ben said, "it's not my firm."

"It's got your name on the sign."

"I'm a partner, Pops." He opted not to mention that he'd discussed stepping back for the foreseeable future. He would still do projects and be a part of the firm, but he wasn't spending whatever time his grandfather had left focused on expanding the business and working sixteen-hour days.

Turning thirty-seven with a major breakup under his belt had been a hard wake-up call about where his life was and where it was heading.

He wanted a family. A home. A life. His gaze settled on his grandfather. Their lives had fallen apart when Ben's father had disappeared thirty years ago, and things hadn't been right since. Ben had gone on with his life, sure. But not the life he heard his grandfather speak about. The real family where you did things together. You built a home life and a work life that were woven together with love and time spent together.

He wanted that.

And he wanted his grandfather to be around to see that it could still be done.

"Seems to me," Ward said, leaning back in his chair and cradling his coffee mug, "they'd be expecting more from a partner than video conferences and long-distance project management."

So, he'd picked up on what Ben was up to. "I'm not going back to full-time work at the firm, Pops. I'm stepping back in order to build up the family business and to get my personal life in order."

Ward's gaze narrowed. "You found someone around here I don't know about yet? Because this decision sure as heck better not be about taking care of an old man and the fleeting legacy his daddy built."

Ben sipped his coffee for a while before going for the snap. This discussion would need to go down strategically. Like a hard-fought state football championship. Otherwise the opposing team would be closing in for the win.

"No, sir. I haven't found anyone. I haven't been looking. Not really, anyway."

Ward harrumphed. "In my opinion, there's trouble if you aren't looking at all."

"And I'm not giving up anything just because I'm needed around here." He opted to stick with the career decision rather than go down the relationship road. When his grandfather would have said more, Ben interrupted, "This is not solely about you, old man. Mom is fifty-eight. She needs me a little more these days too."

Another of those unimpressed harrumphs sounded.

Yeah, well, he got why his grandfather felt that way, but Lucinda Kane was Ben's mother, and he loved her no matter that she could be judgmental and stubborn and nosy. A lot like the man eyeing him right now.

"I just want to do what's right," Ben admitted. "I'm seeing the decay of family more and more—call me old-fashioned, but I want what you and Mimi had. If I'm lucky enough to find it."

Ward stared into his mug for a time. "Women like your mimi are hard to find." His gaze settled on Ben's. "But they're out there." He exhaled a big breath. "That's an admirable goal. Just don't cut yourself short on the follow-through. You're a good man, Bennett. Just like your daddy was. Any woman would be lucky to have you as a husband. Remember that too."

The smile that tugged at Ben's lips wouldn't be ignored. His grandfather only called him Bennett when he was really serious. His mother had refused to allow her child to be Ward Kane the Third. Instead she'd chosen her maiden name for his given name. The story was that his grandfather hadn't spoken to her for a month after Ben had been born. But Mimi had brought him around. Like he'd said, his mother and his grandfather were the two hardest-headed people he knew.

"I'll keep that in mind," Ben promised. "But in all seriousness, this is what I want. I'll have the work that goes along with that hard-earned degree Mom wanted me to have, but I'll also have this, and I love *this*."

Ward nodded. "You won't get any more argument from me."

Ben was glad to hear it. "So, you'll let me paint the house?" It wasn't that big. Two stories. Three bedrooms, two baths. He could handle it.

"As long as it doesn't get in the way of your search for that special someone."

A strangled laugh burst out of him. "Oh, man. I have a feeling I shouldn't have been so brutally honest."

"Honesty is always the best policy." His grandfather nodded. "In fact, that oldest Burton girl just got divorced. I see her at church with her mama. She's—"

"Pops," he warned, "don't even go there."

"Just trying to give you a hand," Ward suggested.

The buzz of the ancient doorbell saved Ben from having to respond. He slid off his stool. "Finish your coffee—I'll get the door."

"Suit yourself." Ward lifted his mug in a sort of salute.

Ben glanced out the window as he stepped into the front hall. He didn't recognize the vintage Land Rover that sat in the drive next to his truck. The idea that his grandfather hadn't argued about answering the door suddenly pinged him. He already knew who it was. There was one thing most of the older folks around here had in common, he'd noticed: they liked knowing who was at their door or calling their phone. And they liked knowing it first.

If the visitor was the Burton girl, as he'd called her, with a Sunday-afternoon casserole, Ben was not going to be happy. He braced himself and opened the door.

Fiery red hair. It was the first thing that captured his attention.

"Good afternoon," the woman standing before him said.

Green eyes. Ben blinked. Not the Burton woman. "Afternoon, ma'am." Confusion furrowed his brow. He glanced at the Land Rover and then at the lady. Not from around here, for sure. Everyone knew everyone else in a small community like this one. "You lost?"

She smiled. He blinked again. The lady was pretty, for sure, but when she smiled...wow. Okay, so maybe the conversation with his grandfather had left him off balance. This was not his normal reaction to meeting strangers—even gorgeous ones wearing snug jeans and a green sweater that brought out the green in her eyes.

"I hope not." She looked around the porch and then at the front yard before meeting his gaze once more. "I'm here to see Mr. Ward Kane. He's expecting me."

Ben's frown deepened. "Okay." He stepped back and opened the door wider. "Come on in. We were just having coffee in the kitchen."

She stepped inside, and he closed the door behind her. She surveyed the front hall, studied the staircase and the line of photos that marched up the wall to the second floor. He hadn't looked at the place from a stranger's viewpoint in forever. Natural wood floors. The matching wood treads of the staircase were worn from time and use. Plaster walls that pushed up to ten feet where an ancient ceiling fan turned slowly—its only speed. It was a well-loved and timeworn home.

He gestured for her to go ahead of him. "Right through there."

These old center-hall farmhouses were mostly all the same. The staircase and a wide welcoming area split the downstairs in half. On the left was the parlor, or living room. On the right was a dining room. Straight ahead, beyond the stairs with its neatly tucked bathroom, was the kitchen that took up the better part of the area across the back of the house. Next to that was the one downstairs bedroom, which had its own bath that had been added half a century ago.

Upstairs was far smaller with only two bedrooms and a shared bath. But the hall on the second level was broad enough for a small office area or den. That hall also led out onto an upper porch that overlooked the backyard.

The design was nothing like the more space-conscious and elegant designs of today, but it was practical and functional. More importantly, no other place had ever felt like home to him. If he was completely honest with himself, he wanted to raise his future family here in this house.

He banished the thought. He really did need to get his brain on track and off his current single status. It wasn't like time was running out for him to find someone. In his entire life, he could not remember ever being this totally preoccupied with not being in a relationship.

When they entered the kitchen, Ward had cleared away the coffee mugs, and a pitcher of lemonade and three glasses sat on the big table they used for casual eating as well as for a workspace, much like modern islands. Stools lined two sides.

"Miss Hart," Ward said with a broad smile. "I hope you had no trouble finding me."

The two met in the center of the room and shook hands.

"Your directions were spot-on." She surveyed the room. "You have a lovely home, Mr. Kane."

"No, no," he argued. "You call me Ward."

"You should call me Reyna."

While his grandfather gushed, Ben did a double take when his gaze landed on the plate of cookies sitting just beyond the pitcher and glasses. What in the world was this about? His grandfather did not bake. A quick glance around the counter and Ben spotted the white box from Sweet Feed, the local bakery. Since the shop wasn't open on Sundays, he'd had to pick up the cookies on Saturday—which meant he'd had this appointment scheduled for at least a day.

Something like denial twisted with irritation started a climb up Ben's spine. If this was some sort of matchmaking—

"This is my grandson, Ben."

He snapped from the thought and looked from his grandfather to the woman.

"It's a pleasure to meet you as well, Ben." She thrust her hand in his direction. "I genuinely appreciate your time."

His hand wrapped around hers. Small, soft… Warmth flashed through his senses. "I'm afraid I'm at a loss here."

Reyna Hart looked from Ben to Ward, but before she could question his confusion, his grandfather said, "Sit, please. I made fresh lemonade, and those cookies are the best in the county." The grin on his lips softened the edge of frustration closing in on Ben. "Storytelling," his grandfather went on, "calls for lemonade and cookies."

Storytelling?

Reyna settled on a stool, and Ward poured the lemonade. Watching in a sort of dismay that had him feeling as if he wasn't actually here and was seeing this from someplace else, Ben took a stool and waited for the other shoe to drop.

As soon as he'd placed glasses of lemonade in front of their visitor and Ben, Ward picked up a cookie and took a bite, then hummed his approval. "No one makes a chocolate chip cookie like Carol McVee."

"That sounds like a challenge to me," their guest proposed as she snagged a cookie of her own and took a bite. "Hmm. You may be right, Ward. This is excellent."

Ben could only stare.

As if she'd picked up on his confusion, Reyna turned in his direction. "Your grandfather has kindly agreed to help me with my research on the Whispering Winds Widows."

Her words landed like a blow to his gut. He flinched. "Research?"

She nodded. "Yes. I'm a writer, and I would very much like to solve the mystery that surrounds the disappearance of the Three."

Now he got it. He laughed, but the sound was far from pleasant. "So you hope to do what no one else has been able to do in thirty years?" He laughed again, couldn't help himself. "What dozens—and I mean dozens—of other people, cops, PIs, investigative reporters, have tried to do. To no avail?"

Ben paid no attention to the glower his grandfather was sending his way.

Her head dipped in a slow nod. "Yes, I hope to do exactly that. Is talking today going to be a problem?" She looked from Ben to Ward. "If so, I can come back at another time."

"It is not an issue," Ward said firmly, with an equally hard look in Ben's direction. "No one wants the truth about what happened to my son more than me and Ben. Isn't that right?"

For most of his adult life, Ben had pretended his father had died—since there had never been any other explanation and he hadn't come back and no body had been found. What else was a kid to do? His mother had refused to speak of what had happened. She'd had no choice in the beginning while the official investigation had been in full swing. But after that she'd never spoken of what had happened or of her missing husband. Ever. It was like she wanted to erase the memories so she no longer had to feel the pain.

If Lucinda Kane were in this room right now, she would simply walk out. She wouldn't ask questions, wouldn't shout her frustrations or anger—she'd just go. By the time Ben had left for college, he had pretty much taken that same path. God knew he'd asked enough questions and done enough digging himself, once he'd been old enough. But no amount of wondering or digging or feeling sorry for himself had ever changed one thing.

His father and two other men—his friends—had vanished, never to be heard from again.

That had been thirty years ago.

His mother had a point. Always looking back and wondering was too hard. It was far easier just to look forward and not think about it.

Before his brain could catch up with his mouth, Ben was nodding and saying in answer to his grandfather's question, "No one."

This woman—this stranger, a writer who wanted to delve into his most painful past—smiled brightly. Her green eyes flashed vibrantly. Her cheeks flushed the tiniest bit. "That's great. I can't tell you how much I'm looking forward to working with the two of you. This is such an important endeavor."

The two of them? He glanced at his grandfather. What had he promised this woman?

"Do you work for a newspaper or other media outlet?" The question had only just bobbed to the surface through all the disbelief and confusion fogging Ben's brain. His gut was in knots, his chest tight enough to bust open like an overinflated tire.

"No. I'm an independent writer. This is a story that I want to write, but before I can do that, I need to find the facts."

This just got worse. This woman intended to write the story of the Widows and the Three. His mother would go ballistic, even if only inside, where no one else could see or hear. Right or wrong as to how she looked at the past, Lucinda Kane was Ben's mother and he had an obligation to look out for her.

"If you're expecting me to help with this in any way, you should know I won't go down any path that puts my mother in a bad light."

Reyna nodded her understanding, her eyes searching his. "I would never expect you to disparage or hurt your mother in any way. Whatever you think of the people who've tried to solve this mystery, I'm not here to find what I want at all costs. I'm not that sort of person. I'm here to find the truth…if I can. Your and your grandfather's help will go a long way in guiding my search in the right directions. I look forward to your input and your oversight."

As much as part of him wanted to argue, to question her seemingly carefully laid-out sincerity, he couldn't bring himself to do it. There was something about her. Not just the way she maintained direct eye contact or the way she stuck to her guns about wanting to do this right… but the genuine passion he heard in her voice. All of it coalesced into something he couldn't ignore. Couldn't deny wanting to see through. Not to mention that he didn't want to embarrass his grandfather by refusing to help.

"All right." He gave a nod. "We can start first thing in the morning." He glanced at his grandfather. "Works better for my schedule, actually."

A frown lined her pretty face and punctuated the scattering of freckles across the bridge of her nose. "Why not start now?"

"Because I need to find out exactly who you are, and when we start, in the morning," he repeated, "we'll start with who my father was and go from there."

"All right, then." Challenge rose in her eyes. "Name the place and time, and I'll see you in the morning." She looked to his grandfather. "If that's all right with you, Ward. We can reschedule our interview." Her gaze returned to Ben. "I wouldn't want anyone to be uncomfortable."

"Works just fine for me," the older man assured her. The tightness in his voice warned he was not happy about his grandson's reaction.

Ben gave her a nod then. "We'll meet at eight sharp at the old Henry place on Shadow Brook Lane."

She scooted off her stool and thrust out her hand for another shake—maybe to seal the deal. "I'll be there."

Ben gripped her hand tightly. "See you then."

He released her hand, and she stepped back. "I can see myself out."

When the front door had closed behind her, his grandfather swung a glare in his direction. "Are you really planning on making her talk to you while you're renovating that old house? For God's sake, boy, it's a mess over there."

Ben shrugged. "You can serve her lemonade and cookies when she interviews you, if that makes you happy, Pops. But if she wants to know about the Kane family from me, then she'll follow me around and see with her own eyes what we're about."

"If you don't want to be a part of this," Ward argued, "just say so, but don't try these antics in hopes of running her off—because I do want to be a part of it."

That was the part that hit Ben the wrong way. "Why? What makes you believe for a second that she can find anything no one else has? Do you even know her?"

He nodded. "You're damn straight I know her. Eudora Davenport sent her. If Eudora trusts her, then I trust her."

"Ms. Davenport is very ill, Pops. We can't be sure she knows what this woman is all about."

"You can help me with this," his grandfather growled, "or you can stay out of the way. I want the truth."

He started clearing the table.

Ben didn't move. Couldn't move.

The sudden urge to have things repaired when Ben had been on him for months to let him do the maintenance that needed to be taken care of hit like a punch to the gut. The decision to paint the house. Holy crap.

"Are you sick, Pops?"

His grandfather glared at him. "What I am is old.

Eighty-five. I won't live forever, boy. I want the truth before I go."

The decision came swiftly and profoundly. No way in the world would he stand in the way of something his grandfather clearly wanted this badly. "I've never tried to figure it out," Ben admitted. "Not really. Not with real effort. Let's face it—whenever I have tried talking to Mom, she cuts me off. You and Mimi were too deep into the search for the truth to have time to figure out how I could fit in."

Hurt passed over the older man's face. "That was never our intent, Ben. We were devastated. We couldn't see beyond finding him…at least for a long while."

"That wasn't a criticism, Pops. It was just the way it felt. I knew even then that the two of you were doing the best you could. The way I survived all of it was to, in time, let it go. Leave it to the reporters and cops who from time to time developed an interest. To go on with my life."

But had he? Was he really any different from his mother or his grandparents? Had he really, deep down, let go?

Maybe not. Maybe that was why he hadn't been able to hang on to the relationship with his ex-fiancée. How could you move forward with the now if part of you was still mired in the past?

Ben took the three strides that separated him from his grandfather and hugged him. When he drew back, he gave the old man a nod. "We will find the truth. No matter what it takes, and if this Reyna Hart can help us, then I'm all in."

The emotion that shone in his grandfather's eyes was all the confirmation Ben needed to know he'd made the right decision.

The strangest sensation—a bit of anticipation mixed with something a little like fear—welled inside him.

Thirty years was a long time to wait for the truth. He just hoped that truth wasn't more painful than not knowing.

Chapter Three

Henry Property
Shadow Brook Lane
Monday, April 22, 8:00 a.m.

The old Henry place, as Mr. Kane had called it, was just that—old and run-down. But like the other old places Reyna had seen in the area, it had a loveliness about it. When restored it would be the sort of farmhouse seen on television renovation programs.

Reyna put the Land Rover in Park and shut off the engine. She'd spoken to Eudora at length last night. She'd asked all sorts of questions about the town and the people Reyna had met so far. Not so many, really. Just Birdie Jewel at the B and B and Mr. Ward and his grandson.

She imagined he—the grandson—was in there looking out a window now. He obviously wasn't happy she was here. Not that she could blame him, really. She'd scoured the internet for stories about the Widows and the missing husbands. So much of what had been published about the families cast a negative light on them. Though no evidence of foul play on the part of any of the three families had been found, doubt, suspicion and accusations had been all over the place.

How was it that all three Widows had remained single and living right where they'd been when their husbands had disappeared? Even Reyna couldn't deny the oddity of that reality thirty years later. The possibility that one or more of the Widows knew some little something that could break the case was possible, maybe even probable. Yet for three decades their stories had remained the same without deviation.

Reyna wondered, if one were to become terminally ill, would that change?

Not that she wished any such thing, of course, but it would be interesting to see what happened at that point.

For now, Reyna thought as she reached for the car-door handle, she would try this the old-fashioned way—with hard work and a heavy dash of relentlessness.

She really hadn't come prepared for this sort of endeavor like this morning's meeting in a renovation project, but between her and Birdie, she'd pulled together something to wear. Her hiking shoes and the jeans she'd brought along were fine, but she hadn't bothered with any casual-work sorts of shirts. Birdie had lent her a couple of sweatshirts that were perfect for this cool day. The fact that the sweatshirts sported logos of flowers and birds suited Reyna just fine. She had a feeling that beneath all her exotic jewelry and flowing clothing, Ms. Birdie Jewel was an old hippie at heart.

By the time Reyna reached the steps, Ben was waiting for her on the porch.

"Morning," he said with one of those male nods that you had to be looking for to spot.

"Good morning to you." She climbed the final step and set her hands on her hips. "Why don't you show me around the place and tell me what your reno involves?"

He shrugged. The movement involved only one shoulder and was nearly as negligent as the nod. "Or we could just get straight to the point as to the relevance of this house to your research. This house was the last place the Three were known to be together. No one saw them here that day, of course. But the wives all stated that there was a meeting here."

He gestured to the door, and she went inside.

Reyna was surprised at his bluntness and to find lights on inside. Though there would have been some light anyway since it was morning, the interior would have been shadowed without interior illumination.

"I had temporary power restored on Friday," he explained, noting her attention to the vintage fixtures hanging from the ceilings and the sconces on the wall near the fireplace.

Reyna wandered to the staircase. It was a bit more ornate than she'd expected for a farmhouse. The flower carvings on the newel-post were particularly interesting. She traced the surface, her fingers noting the slight irregularities in the pattern that suggested it had been hand carved. The front edge of the treads reflected the same carefully hand-carved design.

"My father and grandfather's work."

Reyna turned to Ben. "Your father worked in the city," she said, not arguing with him but surprised by the information.

"The summer before he disappeared," Ben began, "my father left his job in the city and started working with my grandfather again. My mother was most unhappy. She had bigger plans than Whispering Winds and hoped to move down to the city in time."

So there had been trouble with at least one of the couples. The three men had disappeared on October first—the upcoming October would be thirty-one years ago. It had been a Saturday, and the men had met here at this house for a card game. They'd played cards twice a month. Had for years. To anyone's knowledge, nothing had been different or amiss that time except for the meeting place. Considering that it was well away from the men's homes, privacy might have been the motivating factor.

Reyna turned around in a slow circle, taking in the front hall and the parlors on either side. She let the idea that this was the place where they'd met up for the very last time on that fateful day soak in.

"Who owned this house at the time?" Reyna asked, moving to the parlor on the left side of the hall. The mirrored overmantel of the fireplace was dusty but in perfect condition. Even the tile around the firebox looked great.

"Duke Fuller. He and his wife, Deidre, wanted to restore the home and turn the farm back into a thriving property. Deidre didn't care for the plain details, so she hired my grandfather to add a few distinctive ones. Like the carving on the staircase." He gestured to the fireplace. "And the overmantel."

Judging by the condition and the layers of dust, Reyna assumed the house had remained empty all these years. "The restoration was never finished?"

"No. Deidre left it just as it was, and it sat here all this time. She decided to put the place on the market and asked me to get it back in shape."

"You have a team or a couple of employees?" Otherwise this was going to be a long wait for the lady.

Ben laughed. "Just me and my pops, though there isn't a lot he can do these days. I have a few sources—friends—who help out from time to time if the need arises."

"I guess it's a good thing she's not in a rush, then." Reyna moved back into the front hall and crossed to the other parlor.

"Guess so," he agreed.

Reyna didn't wait for an invitation; she moved on to the kitchen that spanned the back of the house. The layout of the first floor was very similar to the one at the Kane home, with the exception of no bedroom downstairs. The only other room on the first floor was a smaller parlor that, considering all the bookshelves lining the walls, had been a library.

"There was no blood or other evidence of violence found in the house or anywhere outside," she said.

"Nothing," he agreed.

"What was the overall condition of the house at the time?" Reyna searched her memory for the details. "No one had lived in it for a number of years, correct?"

"That's right." He crossed to a broad window and stared out over the landscape. "The Henry family had all died out, and the place had been empty for about fifteen years. It was in pretty good shape. Just needed an update and whatever options the new owners wanted to add."

"Was there any connection between Ms. Fuller and the previous owners?" Deidre Fuller's maiden name was Henry.

"The last owner was her uncle," Ben said. "He had no children, and when he passed, the property went to Deidre. She was a teenager at the time, so her parents held it in trust for her. Judging by some of the photographs I've found in my mother's old scrapbooks, they used this place as a hangout a lot in their younger days."

"Before they married?"

"Right. Like a private teenage hangout."

And then their husbands had disappeared here. In Reyna's opinion, that had to mean something.

"I know what you're thinking," Ben said. He leaned against one of the bookcases, arms crossed over his chest. "I'm sure you read how about ten years ago ground-penetrating radar was brought in. They found no remains anywhere on the property. Not in the garden, not in the basement. Nowhere. The properties where the Three lived were checked as well."

She had read the articles. A private investigator with his own television program had talked his producers into paying for the venture. Deidre Fuller had agreed to the only interview she'd done in twenty years. Reyna guessed because it would be part of the episode to air on television. Who didn't love that fifteen minutes of fame? Although, in Deidre's case, it had been more like three minutes. The main focus had been on the search for remains.

"THERE'S NOTHING HERE," Ben said, "that's going to tell the story of what happened that day." This might not be true, but whatever was here, he wanted to be the one to find it.

Truth was he and Ms. Fuller had made a deal. He'd bought the place from her. No one was to know. He didn't want his mother or his grandfather to know, and she didn't want the public stir that would've surely followed the sale. So they'd executed a private transaction. He'd used the firm's little-known development company to buy the property so no one would easily attach his name to it.

At this point he wasn't really sure why he'd done it. Maybe it was reaching that age where life felt as if it were slipping by or maybe it was the breakup, but he'd suddenly needed desperately to do something. To figure out the past. To force it all to make sense somehow. Though he was fairly confident it never would.

But for some reason he had to try.

He hadn't quite determined the reason, but he intended to do all in his power to get it done.

The idea that it perhaps had something to do with his grandfather's advanced age wasn't lost on him. The realization shook him, though this was not the first time he'd considered losing the man who had been his rock, his mentor—his world for most of his life. Ben did not want his grandfather to die never knowing what happened to his son. It just wasn't right.

Clearly the man wanted to know or he wouldn't have agreed to work with this…Reyna Hart.

His gaze settled on her as she wandered around the room looking at empty shelves as if the dust settled there might give her some insight.

He shook his head. How the hell would he get this done?

Reyna turned to face him. He flinched. The curiosity that captured her expression warned she hadn't missed his lingering attention. To cover, he said, "What's going through your mind right now?" He shrugged. "I mean, you're not from around here. You don't know any of the folks involved. You're not a cop or a reporter. What does all this—" he turned his arms up "—say to you?"

She walked around the room, did a little more looking at the dust and cobwebs because God knew there was nothing else.

"It says there are secrets," she announced, stopping maybe three feet away. Close enough for him to see those little freckles that made him want to trace their faint path.

He chuckled, mostly to cover the ridiculous thought about those freckles that had popped into his head. "I hate to tell you this, Miss Hart, but that's hardly original and definitely not news."

She gave him an acknowledging nod. "However, the point you're missing, Mr. Kane, is that there are secrets and then there are *secrets*."

His gaze narrowed as he searched her face, looking for some hint of where she was going with this. "I'm listening."

"We all have secrets. Little things we do or say or that happen which we want to keep to ourselves. A little something we did or a habit that isn't flattering. A mistake we made. That sort of thing."

He got it now. "But you're saying the secret or secrets about the Three is a different kind. The sort that has to stay secret no matter what. The kind that turns worlds upside down." The twist in his gut told him she was right about that.

She nodded. "Exactly. Someone knows something. Someone right here in this little town. Someone you probably know. Maybe one or all of the Widows. And this thing they know could potentially reveal everything or just the first step in the right direction."

"But how do you find that…thing?"

"You ask the right people the right questions, and you keep looking. It's here. It has to be. It's basic physics. All things that exist must be somewhere. The bodies—if the Three are dead—are somewhere. The weapon—if they were murdered—is somewhere. The murderer is somewhere."

"All right." Made sense so far. "I'll tell you now I've searched this house top to bottom. I've walked this property step by step. I've found nothing."

"Not finding it doesn't mean it's not there," she countered. "What it means is that you need additional direction. The only way to get the right additional direction is to go to the source."

"The Widows."

"Yes. They were married to the missing men. They knew them and each other better than anyone—intimately—since they were lifelong friends. One or all of them knows something that can help us. All we need is a point in the right direction. We need at least one to give us that direction."

The need to protect his mother nudged him. "You're saying one or all three of the Widows have been lying all this time."

"Not necessarily. It's possible that she or they don't understand the importance of what is known. Or it could be fear. Until you know why the three husbands went missing, you won't know the motive for keeping the knowledge secret. And there will be a motive. Does that motive pose some sort of threat to the Widows? Who's to say? But that is the typical reason secrets are kept."

The idea wasn't a new one. It had been discussed in previous investigations, but nothing had ever come of it. One investigator had even gone so far as to say that until it was known why the Three had disappeared there would never be any other answers.

Evidently, he'd made a valid point. Thirty years felt a whole hell of a lot like *never* at this point.

"You want me to get you meetings with the Widows," Ben suggested.

"Your grandfather has already offered to do this, but if you'd rather be the one to make it happen, I can work with that."

His mother would say no. He knew this up front. Ms. Fuller might be eager to get her point of view in first.

She'd been easy to talk to when Ben had purchased the property. Then again, money had been involved. She might not feel the same when it wasn't. He couldn't say how Ms. Evans would react, but he was willing to try to make it happen.

"I'll get the meetings," he agreed. "While I work that out, how about I take you on a tour of the property and then our town. You'll have a better understanding of the place and the people then."

"I would really appreciate that. Believe it or not, getting the feel of a place and the people can often sharpen your instincts."

"I can see that." Made sense.

Funny, he hadn't expected to like this woman. The very last thing he'd wanted was someone else involved in what he felt he had to do.

Now it seemed exactly like the right move.

Then again, it wouldn't be the first time he'd made a mistake.

Chapter Four

Harold's Diner
Main Street
Noon

Reyna liked this town already. Small, quiet. Everyone seemed to know everyone else. Then again, she had been hearing about it from Eudora for months. Reyna felt at home here because of all that she'd learned and studied about the place. She'd spent so much time thinking about it, it was as if she'd lived here herself.

The reality of it, though, was even nicer than her expectations. The real place felt…peaceful.

This conclusion felt a bit strange since a possible triple homicide had taken place thirty years ago that remained unsolved. How was it that three grown men had vanished in a town so small and no one had a clue what had happened?

There was no logic in the notion.

Reyna studied the man seated across the table from her. Ben Kane's father had been one of those three. How had he gone on through life all this time and not fought harder to know the reason? Then again, perhaps he had. Eudora had said little about Ben. She'd mostly spoken about his grandfather, Ward. Reyna suspected the two had had a connection at one time—perhaps a brief affair after his wife had passed away. A retired schoolteacher, Eudora had never been married. She had no children.

Ben looked up from the menu he'd been perusing. "If you've got a question, the best thing to do is ask it. Staring a hole through me isn't going to get you any answers."

"Why now?" she asked. "In the past I'm sure you've followed along with the investigations. Maybe even been involved on some level, but why decide to go the extra mile, so to speak, now?"

And that was the impression he'd given when he'd shown her around the Henry property. He wanted very much to find the truth. She had felt the tension in him when he'd spoken of his grandfather's pain all these years, of how the disappearance had certainly sent his grandmother to an early grave.

Whatever his mother wanted, he hadn't mentioned. Reyna suspected, based on Eudora's conclusions about the Widows, that none of them wanted the past shaken or stirred ever again.

The trouble in that was this man—and Reyna. They both wanted answers. This wasn't personal for her. She didn't really know these people or this community, but it felt important. It felt like something she needed to do.

Ben placed the menu on the table. Reyna hadn't even really looked at hers. She wasn't hungry for anything except answers.

He held her gaze for long enough to have her wondering if he intended to answer. Finally he said, "My grandfather is eighty-five. His health is really good, in my opinion, for a man of his age. That said, I can't deny the idea that I could lose him anytime. I know he wants answers. He tried harder than most to get those answers before admitting defeat. If I can somehow find those answers, it would be the most important thing I could possibly do for him. I want to do that for him."

Reyna smiled and gave him a nod. "I can't imagine a more noble reason."

A gray-haired gentleman wearing an apron with the diner logo swaggered up to their booth. "Afternoon, folks." He nodded to Ben. "You ready to order?"

Ben eyed him skeptically. "Since when did you start taking orders, Harold?"

Ah, Reyna got it now. This was the owner, Harold McGill. Eudora had said he was a very generous man—always feeding and taking up donations for those in need.

"Well now, Ben," Harold said as he eyed the two of them, "that would be your fault for waltzing in here with this pretty stranger. You're gonna have the whole town talking."

"It doesn't take much," Ben said under his breath.

She smiled and reached out to the older man. "Reyna Hart. It's a pleasure to meet you, Mr. McGill. I've heard wonderful things about you from Eudora Davenport."

"Mercy me." McGill grinned. "I hope she's doing well. I haven't seen Eudora in ages."

"She's doing well enough," Reyna said. Eudora wasn't keen on anyone knowing the extent of her illness. "In fact, one of the projects I'm working on is Eudora's life history."

McGill's eyebrows reared up. "Now, that's a story I'd love to read. They say still waters run deep, and Eudora Davenport's ran deeper than most, in my opinion."

"I'm including the mystery of the Widows and their missing husbands as well."

His expression turned to one of surprise as he glanced at Ben. "Is that so?" He pursed his lips and nodded. "It'd be a good thing, I suppose, to finally know what happened all those years ago."

"You knew my dad pretty well," Ben said. "Anything come to mind about that time frame? Any sort of trouble or issues?"

To Reyna's surprise, the older man walked over to a table, grabbed an empty chair and dragged it to the end of their booth. He settled his short, stout frame into it and propped his elbows on the table. "Your daddy," he said to Ben, "was a good man. Better than most, I'd wager. Just like his own daddy."

"You going to take their order or wag your tongue?"

Reyna shifted her attention to the woman who now stood behind McGill. She had the same gray hair as the owner, but it was twisted high on her head in a bun. The name tag pinned to her uniform said Vinnia. His wife. Reyna recognized the name.

"Ben'll take the cheeseburger plate," McGill said. "With a glass of water."

Ben nodded. Obviously the man knew his preferred lunch.

"The lady…" McGill turned to Reyna.

"Will take the same," she filled in for him. "Reyna Hart," she added for Ms. McGill's benefit.

"I'd ask what brings you to our town," Vinnia said as she scratched the orders onto her notepad, "but I couldn't help overhearing the subject of the conversation."

Reyna doubted that was the case since the diner was busy and hummed with conversation in addition to the soft music from a local radio station playing from the speakers. Most of the customers were crowded around the counter and spread around the diner far enough away from the booth Ben had chosen to give them some amount of privacy. If Vinnia had overheard anything it was because she'd made the extra effort.

"We'd love to hear your thoughts as well," Reyna offered.

"I don't imagine Ben would care for my thoughts," the older woman said with a glance in his direction. "He knows how I feel about his mama."

Ben mustered up a smile—a charming one in spite of the woman's attitude. Reyna was impressed.

"I also know the feeling is mutual on my mother's side."

Vinnia shot Reyna a look. "You see, that's why we'll never have the whole story on what happened. Those Widows are keeping it to themselves. Whatever you hope to find, Ms. Hart, I'd start with Lucinda Kane. She's the one who started it all."

Before Reyna could respond, the lady twisted around and hurried away.

Ben said nothing. McGill's face had gone red.

"You'll have to overlook my wife," he said. "She has a sore spot where your mama is concerned, Ben. That's not news to you."

"No, sir," he agreed. "It is not."

McGill pushed back his chair and stood. "You two enjoy your lunch, and if I can help in any way, just let me know."

He returned the borrowed chair and disappeared behind the counter.

Reyna gave Ben a minute to comment. When he didn't, she asked, "You want to tell me about it?"

"My mother was engaged to Vinnia's younger brother before she married my father."

Now, there was a detail Reyna hadn't heard. "So there was bad blood between your father and Vinnia's brother?"

"Gordon Walls. He's a Hamilton County sheriff's deputy. There was bad blood, yes. But that was eight years before the disappearance. There hadn't been any trouble during my parents' marriage."

The other man's occupation cued up a whole other line of questioning. "Was Gordon Walls a deputy back then—during the time of the breakup with your mother?"

"He was in the Army. They were supposed to get married when he came back from training, but she married my father before that happened. Walls did his time in the military, then joined the sheriff's department."

"How long was he in the military?" Reyna's instincts were buzzing. She couldn't believe she'd missed this aspect of the story—if it had come up during the numerous investigations. She was certain it hadn't been part of anything she'd read.

"Six years."

Reyna added the information to her mental files and moved on. "Where is Gordon Walls now?"

"He married. Had a family. He and his wife live in Chattanooga."

"What are the chances I can get that interview with your mother today?" Reyna was itching to do some looking into this new aspect of the story and then to approach Lucinda Kane about it.

"I'll talk to her after we're finished here." He glanced at the woman behind the counter, who quickly looked away. Vinnia had been watching them since she'd taken their order. "But I'll need to speak with her alone first."

"I understand. I have other names to follow up on."

He held her gaze for a long moment before saying more.

"I wonder if finding the truth will actually give anyone peace."

Reyna wished she could assure him it would. But it might not. It might create more pain and more questions. But if he wanted to know, now was the time. The window of opportunity was closing. The players, and even the bystanders, from thirty years ago were getting older. Many were already gone.

Before long, there would be no one left who might actually know the answers or may have witnessed something relevant. Better to ask now than wish he had later.

Owens Residence
Rushing Stream Hollow
1:30 p.m.

Retired sheriff's deputy Nelson Owens had been sitting in a rocking chair on his front porch when Reyna had arrived. He had invited her to have a seat in the matching rocking chair. His home was a rustic cabin, well off the road and surrounded by thick woods. He kept a shotgun propped against the railing on the other side of his rocking chair.

She supposed there were all manner of wildlife in those woods. Having a shotgun nearby was likely a good idea. At his age, seventy-one, he probably had no desire to try outrunning a bear or any other predator. Better to scare them off.

He'd offered her a beer, but she'd declined. He'd had several already. Emptied and crushed cans lay in the corner, a few feet from where he sat. Whether this was his daily ritual or just the way he'd braced for her visit, she didn't know. As much as she would like to video all her interviews, she had found that the request generally put people off. So, she didn't take the risk. Better to take notes during or immediately after.

"We never found anything," he said in answer to her question. "It was really strange, if you ask me. Tarrence Norwood, he was the sheriff at the time—a good one, at that—he really tried to find answers. It just never happened."

"Everything I've read says there was no evidence found. No motives for anyone having wanted one or all three of the men gone," she said, recalling the words of the then sheriff. The few television interviews she had seen had shown a deeply, deeply disappointed man for having not been able to solve the case.

Owens shook his head. "It was the strangest thing. You know, usually you find something, hear a rumor or what have you. But we got nothing. Zero. It was like they just vanished. An alien abduction."

There had been plenty of speculation on that one over the years.

"You didn't find anything or hear anything from anyone you interviewed that prompted you to form any sort of scenario? Sometimes we don't have evidence, but we have ideas," she suggested.

He popped the top on another can, took a long swallow. "It's been thirty years," he said. "A lot of people have moved away. Others have died. And no one has ever figured out what the heck happened." Another swallow of beer. "But I'm gonna tell you something I've never told anyone before."

Reyna held her breath, hoped this was a true lead.

"I think the Widows know exactly what happened." He shrugged. "Heck, they might even have killed them. Seems strange to me that they still stick together after all this time and they never remarried or moved or anything else." He frowned at Reyna. "Don't you find that weird?"

"We all have our own way of grieving. Maybe theirs was to do exactly as they've done."

Another shrug. "Maybe. Just seems strange to me. Truth be told, most people around town think they're a little on the odd side."

"Why do *you* think they know what happened?"

"The next day after they disappeared," he explained, "the first call came from Lucinda Kane. She said she was worried because her husband never came home. We went out to see her, and she was so calm. It was like she was saying all the right words. That she was worried and that he'd never done this before...but she didn't seem worried or upset. She was just, you know, normal."

Reyna wondered if Ben was aware of his mother's behavior during the interview. "Perhaps she was in shock."

"Why? At that point we didn't know they weren't coming back. You'd think she would have been worried about an accident or something. She never went out looking for him. Nothing. Most people would have been driving around or calling people, you know."

"Are you sure she didn't?" Reyna certainly wanted his thoughts on the matter, but it was difficult to tell whether this was an opinion based on what had been happening or his perception of what should have been happening.

"We asked if she'd called the local hospitals or friends or looked for him at all, and she just said no. Not one additional detail. Just no."

The reaction was a little odd, she supposed. "When did the next call come in?"

"While we were interviewing Lucinda, Harlowe Evans called, all freaked out. Now, she had been out driving around. She'd called all the hospitals, driven out to the Henry place and called the other wives. That was the reaction you'd expect."

Reasonable point. "What about Ms. Fuller? When did her call come in?"

"Now, that's the really strange one." He opened another can of beer. "She didn't call. We went to her place and asked if her husband had been home. She said no, and then we asked her if that was out of the ordinary for him to leave and not come back. She just shook her head, said she didn't know what was going on."

"Did you or Sheriff Norwood have any reason to believe one or more of the wives were lying?"

He considered the question through two more deep slugs of beer. Then he said, "I always thought there was something Dede Fuller wasn't telling. Deidre," he clarified. "Most everyone calls her Dede. Anyway, she just didn't act right through any of it. She seemed zoned out or something. Maybe shock like you said, but I don't know. The truth is it was all just weird. All of it."

"Looking back," Reyna said, "is there anything you would do differently?"

Another extended consideration. "If I could go back, I'd watch those women day and night. I'd push them harder until one of them cracked."

Interesting answer, Reyna decided. "You're that certain that at least one of them was and still is hiding something."

He looked directly at her then. "I would bet my life on it. If you want to know what happened, that's where you'll find the answer."

He had little else to say after that. Reyna left one of her cards with him and urged him to call if he thought of anything else that might be helpful to her research.

As she drove away, she considered that he was likely right about the Widows, and she had every intention of finding whatever any of them was hiding.

Kane Residence
Thistle Lane
1:50 p.m.

BEN SAT ON the front steps of his childhood home for a while. His mother was inside and no doubt had noticed his arrival. She hadn't come to the door and wouldn't until he rang the bell.

She wasn't happy about his decision to stay in Whispering Winds. She'd been happier when he'd been in the city, focused on building his career. She wanted him to get married and have grandchildren for her to enjoy.

She wanted him to never look back.

Not such an easy task, all things considered.

With a heavy breath, he got up, crossed the porch and knocked on the door. Putting it off any longer wouldn't make it any easier.

She opened the door after his first knock. Oh, yeah, she'd been standing there watching and waiting. Didn't seem right that they had to have this standoff about his being back in Whispering Winds or the past.

She should want to know the whole truth. Maybe if he'd pushed harder when he'd been younger. He shook off the idea. Wouldn't have mattered even then. She had not wanted to discuss it. She had wanted to move on and pretend it was not relevant to the future.

A wide smile spread across Lucinda Kane's face. Even as she headed toward sixty, she was still a beautiful woman who liked taking care of herself, who liked looking nice.

Not a single strand of gray was allowed to survive in her dark mane. Her eyes and hair were the only features he'd gotten from her. Folks said he looked exactly like his daddy except for his mama's blue eyes and black hair.

"What're you up to, Ben?" She opened the door wide and gestured for him to come on in. "You're usually busy with work this time of the afternoon."

He stepped inside, waited for her to close the door. "We need to have a conversation about…things."

Her smile faded instantly. "Have you had lunch? I made a fresh pitcher of iced tea, if you're thirsty."

"No, ma'am," he said. "I'd just like to talk."

She inclined her head and gave him that look that said she so, so did not want to go there. "You know I don't like talking about the past. It's too hard. I don't know why no one seems to understand how difficult those years were for me. Shouldn't I be allowed my peace?"

"I know you don't," Ben agreed. "But I need you to do it anyway. And I need you to understand that I'm not backing off this time. I'm sticking with this until I have the answers."

She drew in a big breath. "Well, in that case, I need a drink."

Lucinda Kane had never been much of a drinker. Not even socially. But whenever the subject of her missing—presumed dead—husband came up, she wanted a drink. He supposed he couldn't blame her.

He followed her to the parlor, where she poured a shot of Jack Daniel's into a glass, drank it down and then settled into her favorite chair—the pink one with the rose-colored throw lying across one arm. Growing up, his friends had often ribbed him about all the pink in the house. But his mother loved pink and she loved roses. What was a boy to do?

When he would have kicked off the conversation, she held up a hand. "Don't tell me where to start. Believe me, I know. At the beginning."

He said nothing, just waited. He'd learned from experience that it was best to allow her to do this her own way or she wouldn't do it at all.

She folded her hands in her lap, closed her eyes as if sifting through memories only she could see. "It was a Saturday, October first. There was a new Halloween thing opening that weekend. A corn maze. Something scary that all your friends wanted to do. Your daddy said I should take you because he had to work over at the Henry place and then, of course, he had that silly card game."

Ben's father and his friends, Duke Fuller and Judson Evans, had played cards together since their college days. Twice a month. The games had moved to the old Henry place after the Fullers had bought it. As long as it had been under renovation and unoccupied, the men had had privacy. All three Widows had given the same statement about the reason their husbands had been at the house at the time of their disappearance. But the card table hadn't been set up. No cigars or glasses were around, as there usually would have been. None of the Three had smoked except when they'd played cards; then they'd puffed on cigars and drank whiskey.

"Dad never had any trouble with the others? I mean, surely at some point during their lives they'd had a falling-out."

"Nothing I know about," she said. "No one else could recall any issues either. But then, I suppose there were little things that no one ever heard about."

She wasn't going to like this one. "Gordon Walls couldn't have come back for revenge?"

Surprise flashed across her face. "What?"

"Gordon Walls. The two of you were engaged when he left for the Army. Then you met Dad, and when Gordon came back you were married to him. That couldn't have gone well."

Her glance at the old-fashioned bar cabinet that had stood next to the parlor's French doors for as long as he could remember warned she wished for a second drink.

"No." She fixed her attention on him. "It did not." She took a breath. "I'm going to tell you this once, and then I will never speak of it again."

This was a new tactic. "Okay."

"Gordon was gone for a long time. I was lonely." She shook her head. "I was young. For goodness' sake, I was barely twenty years old. I didn't mean to get involved with your father, but it happened. He and your grandfather came to my parents' house to repair something or the other. I don't even recall what." A smile tugged at her lips even when she obviously did not want to smile. "He was so handsome. I ran into him again at the county fair, and we walked around together. Rode a few rides. Shared some very innocent kisses."

Her eyes closed as if the rest were too difficult to look at. When she opened them once more, there was a shine of emotion that told Ben he'd been right. This was hard for her, and he regretted that it was necessary.

"We started sneaking around, and—" she looked straight into Ben's eyes "—as you are well aware, I found out I was pregnant with you, and so we got married."

"Did you want to get married?"

Her mouth rounded in shock. "Well, of course we wanted to get married. We just hadn't expected to start with being parents first. But," she said firmly, "I was thrilled when you were born, and I have never once regretted it."

"You're certain my father and Walls never fought about this? No harbored resentment or any bitterness?"

"I'm certain there were exchanges between them," she confessed, "but your father never discussed those with me. He and Gordon handled things very discreetly. I'm confident Gordon didn't want to be humiliated any more than he already had been. It was better to work things out quietly. He was away with his commitment to the military for several years after that anyway. When he came back, it was ancient history."

This was the same story his grandfather had relayed. "The one thing that bothers me," Ben explained, "is that he trained to be a member of law enforcement. Meaning he would know how to make people disappear without leaving evidence. Did any of the folks looking into the case really consider him as a potential suspect?"

"Of course. It was utterly humiliating to me, having to go over and over the details of our former relationship. Gordon had his own life by the time your father went missing. Why on earth would he have bothered with ours? Thankfully, Sheriff Norwood kept that irrelevant history out of the official reports or I would have had to go through the same humiliation every time some detective or reporter wanted to poke around."

"I don't know—the need for revenge is a powerful emotion," Ben said bluntly. "Some folks hold on to a grudge longer than others. Maybe it was an accident? Something Walls didn't intend to start, but once it started he couldn't stop it."

"Even if that were the case, why would he have bothered with the others? Certainly Duke and Judson had nothing in that fight."

"Wrong place, wrong time," Ben suggested. "There are a lot of unknowns when it comes to murder, Mom. Whoever did this had a reason. We just don't know what that reason was."

She looked away. "I don't want to talk about this anymore."

Therein lay the problem. "I have a friend. Reyna Hart. She's working with me to find the answers we all need."

Lucinda shook her head. "I don't need any answers. What difference would they make at this point? My God, it's been thirty years."

"I need answers," Ben said gently. "Pops needs answers."

Anger tightened her lips. "I knew you were doing this for him. You've always been more concerned with his happiness than mine."

And so went the ongoing saga of his mother's jealousy of his relationship with his grandfather.

"You should go back to the city, son. Go on with your life. Stop looking back."

"The way you went on with your life?"

It was a low blow, but he couldn't pretend anymore. His mother had lived in this house—the same one she and his father had bought when they'd married—for the past thirty years. To his knowledge, she had never even dated another man.

"Not fair," she argued. "I had a marriage. A man I loved. A child. My life was and still is complete."

He wasn't going to argue the point and upset her further. "I need you to agree to be interviewed by my friend."

He and Reyna didn't really know each other, but if calling her a friend would get his mother to agree, so be it.

And he did like Reyna.

Lucinda frowned, then rubbed her forehead. "I have a headache coming on. Check with me tomorrow. Perhaps I can speak with your friend then."

At least it wasn't a no. "Can I do anything for you, Mom? Make you some tea?"

She drew in a deep breath and managed a smile. "I'll just lie down, and then I'll be fine. Call me in the morning."

"One more question," he said before relenting.

She rubbed at her forehead. "Very well. Ask your question."

"If you knew anything—anything at all—you would tell me, wouldn't you?"

Her expression turned to one of pain. "Of course I would tell you. What a foolish question." His mother rose from her pink chair and left the room.

But it wasn't a foolish question. It was a completely legitimate one.

Ben stood. He figured Reyna was wasting her time interviewing the Widows. They were all going to tell the same story.

He sincerely hoped the reason was because it was true.

Chapter Five

Our Lady of the Mountain
Kings Lane
2:50 p.m.

Father Vincent Cullen had agreed to meet with Reyna at his home at the church he had served for most of his life. Reyna shut off the engine of her Land Rover and surveyed the area. The church was an old one, for sure. Nestled in the woods on the edges of Whispering Winds, the setting offered a sense of calm and serenity. Reyna grabbed her shoulder bag and climbed out of the vehicle, and she shivered a little with the crisp breeze.

Maybe it was more being at a church than the actual temperature this afternoon. Reyna hadn't been inside a church since her grandmother's funeral. It wasn't so much that she was a nonbeliever, more nonpracticing. For now, anyway.

Though Father Cullen was retired, he lived in the small church rectory. The priest currently assigned to the church lived just next door in the church parsonage. According to Eudora, even at ninety years old, Father Cullen helped out from time to time. The parishioners adored him, which was why the church had both a rectory and a parsonage.

No one had wanted to ask Father Cullen to move out, so the parsonage had been acquired.

Father Cullen waited on the steps of the church. "Good afternoon, Ms. Hart."

Reyna extended her hand as she approached the older man. "Thank you so much for taking the time to see me."

"Any friend of Eudora's is a friend of mine." He smiled, and Reyna got a glimpse of the handsome man he had been when Eudora and her friend Birdie had been so enthralled with him.

Reyna wondered if the man realized how many women in the community had been smitten with him.

"If you'll follow me," he said, "we'll have coffee or tea—whichever you like."

"Sounds perfect."

A cobblestone walkway wandered through the landscape, then split, with a narrower portion leading through a grove of high thick hedges and meeting up with a small addition to the church. The rectory, she presumed. Eudora had said it had been added in the 1940s for Cullen's predecessor.

The rectory was a small studio apartment with worn, cozy furnishings and book-lined shelving covering most walls. There was even a small fireplace. A chair, obviously favored by the current resident, sat near the stone fireplace.

"Sit wherever you'd like," he offered as he made his way to the kitchenette. He checked the kettle for water, then turned on the burner. "I'm a tea lover myself. What suits you, Reyna?"

"Tea would be very nice."

As he gathered the cups and saucers, he said, "So you want to talk about the Three, I presume."

Right to the heart of the matter. "I do. Eudora would

very much like for me to figure out what happened thirty years ago. She feels certain you can help."

Vincent Cullen's hair, though gray, remained thick and full. He was tall yet far thinner than in the photos Eudora had shown her. His voice remained strong and clear. Reyna hoped his memory was also. Even so, it was possible he might choose not to share whatever he knew, particularly if that information had been shared in confidence. This man, Reyna understood, could very well know the secrets no one else did.

"Cream and sugar?" The kettle's whistle underscored his question.

"Both, please."

He delivered her tea before preparing his own. When he'd settled into his chair, he rested his gaze on hers. "I wish I could help Eudora find the peace she desires."

Here it came.

"Unfortunately," he went on, "I have no idea what happened thirty years ago."

His answer surprised Reyna. She'd expected the usual response of being bound by the seal of confession.

"No one in the community has ever spoken to you regarding what he or she did or knew?"

"I'm afraid that's the case." He sipped his tea.

Reyna did the same. The peppermint flavor teased her taste buds.

"I'm sorry," he offered. "I should have mentioned that I only keep peppermint tea."

"It's very good," she assured him. "Do you have any personal feelings or conclusions related to what happened that you can share?"

He sipped his tea for a time before placing it on the table next to his chair. "JR—Ward's son—Duke Fuller and

Judson Evans were all very good men. I'd known them since they were born. Judson was the only one whose family didn't attend services here. I knew him through his relationship with JR and Duke. He came often with one or the other. They were popular in high school. Athletes. No trouble that I was ever made aware of."

There was a *but* coming. Reyna heard it in his tone.

"There was," he began, "a restlessness about the Three. They weren't troublemakers or bullies—nothing of that sort. It was as if they were exploding with the need to do something even they couldn't define. An energy, I suppose you'd call it."

"Do you suppose this restlessness could have prompted one of them to delve into territory he might not otherwise have ventured into?" This was the first time she'd heard or read anything that suggested any of the Three might have been poised to mix things up or launch some new something.

Father Cullen lifted his bushy gray eyebrows. "I can't say, of course. Really, anything I offer will be mere speculation. I can only tell you what I sensed, and I sensed a building need to act somehow."

"Were they still coming to mass here at the church fairly regularly?"

"JR was, of course. And Duke occasionally. Christmas and Easter, mostly. But I saw them around town. Spoke in passing quite regularly. I saw more of JR toward the end because he'd returned to work with his father."

"You sensed this restlessness in JR?"

He nodded. "I suppose I could go a bit further where JR was concerned. His family has always belonged to this parish, and it was easy to see that something was not quite right. Whether it was JR's relationship with Duke and Judson or his relationship with his wife, there were ripples in the water, so to speak."

This sounded like more than restlessness.

"Others have said—" Reyna placed her tea on a nearby table "—there was trouble between JR and Deputy Gordon Walls. Did you notice any lingering animosity between the two men?"

A frown furrowed the man's face. "There were rumors, of course. But Ward, JR's father, is a well-respected member of this community. Folks weren't going to say a lot—at least, not out loud."

"Did JR's friends, Duke and Judson, stand on his side of the situation?" Eudora had insisted the Three had stood together through thick and thin. But hers was only one person's perspective on the matter.

"As far as I was aware, yes. Those three always stood together."

"Father Cullen, what is your opinion of what happened to those three young men?" She turned her hands up. "Let's face it, the chances that they simply ran away or disappeared into thin air are basically nonexistent. Something happened to them. I really, really would appreciate your conclusions."

He held her gaze for a moment. "Just between the two of us? No passing my conclusion along to anyone else?"

"If that's what you require," she agreed.

"It's what I would prefer."

Reyna gave a nod. "Then I won't share your conclusions with anyone."

"I think those three got into some sort of trouble and had no idea how to get out. They had no history of trouble. How would they know what to do? If any one of the

Three survived that day, he's in hiding somewhere and will never return."

Reyna couldn't say she saw the situation any other way. "Do you feel that whatever happened was somehow connected to Deputy Walls?"

He smiled, settled deeper into his chair. "Unless you uncover an alternative, it certainly seems the most likely."

From there, the conversation moved on to the weather and local events. Reyna interjected more questions from time to time in hopes Father Cullen would reveal more with his guard down, but she learned nothing she didn't already know. As the conversation wound down, he invited Reyna to mass and urged her to pass his thoughts and prayers on to Eudora.

As she prepared to leave, Reyna gave him one of her business cards. Since he was feeling overly tired, she insisted he not walk her back to where she'd parked. She'd enjoyed meeting him no matter that she'd learned very little from a source who surely knew far more.

She sat in her Land Rover for a time and considered how those three young men had attended services here in this lovely old church. They'd maintained good reputations and been popular among the community.

Yet they had disappeared suddenly and seemingly without warning.

Reyna exited the church parking lot and headed back into Whispering Winds proper. She hoped to hear from Ben soon with news that she could meet with his mother and the other Widows.

Ben's mother had been the least cooperative in interviews over the years. Harlowe Evans appeared to always be up for them. Deidre Fuller had done much the same as Evans, though with less and less frequency over the years. Did that suggest Lucinda Kane had something to hide? Reyna hoped not. She liked Ward and Ben. If Reyna was going to find the truth—and she intended to give it her best shot—she didn't really want it to turn the world even more upside down for the Kane family. But her first loyalty was to Eudora.

Her cell phone rang, and Reyna reached toward the passenger seat for her bag, blindly feeling for the phone in the side pocket. This stretch of highway was far too curvy to take her eyes off the road and risk going over a cliff. The Land Rover suddenly lurched to the right. Reyna whipped the steering wheel to the left in an attempt to correct its path, but she was too late—the wheel slipped off the edge of the pavement. Her heart launched into her throat as she attempted to pull the vehicle back onto the pavement and away from the cliff, which only made matters worse. She pressed harder on the brake, and the Land Rover slid sideways, heading for the tree line.

A scream became stuck in her throat. Reyna fought for control, finally wrestling the vehicle to a complete stop just shy of a massive tree.

She shoved the gearshift into Park and sat for a moment, unable to move or to think. Her whole body shook with the receding adrenaline.

What the devil had happened?

Finally, gathering her wits, she released her seat belt, opened the door and climbed out. Her knees buckled, and she had to catch herself on the door.

Steadying herself, she surveyed the driver's side of the vehicle. No damage. The front end faced the highway away from the trees, so she moved around the back. Nothing on the rear. Thankfully. Squeezing between the Land Rover and the trees on the passenger side wasn't so easy. To her great relief there was no visible damage to that side of the vehicle either.

Except for the flat front tire.

So that was why she'd lost control.

"Damn it." She moved closer and peered down at the tire. Totally flat. She rose up and looked along the highway in both directions.

She needed a tow truck.

Making her way back around to the driver's side, she decided she would call Ben. He would know where she could get the tire repaired and a reliable towing service.

As she plucked her bag from the front passenger-side floorboard, she hoped there was no damage under the vehicle. She did vaguely recall bumping over the ground with some rather sharp jolts and jerks.

"Don't borrow trouble, Reyna," she grumbled as she fished out her cell phone.

This was not how she'd seen her first full day on this venture going.

Ben answered on the first ring. He promised to be there in ten minutes.

Reyna leaned against her crippled vehicle and studied her surroundings.

It really was a beautiful, peaceful place.

How could anyone—much less three full-grown men—just disappear in such a nice place?

Kane Residence
Lula Lake Lane
6:00 p.m.

THE SCENT OF vegetable soup stirred Reyna's appetite, had her stomach vying for attention.

"Mr. Kane," she said, "you really don't have to go to all this trouble."

Ward Kane shot her a look from his position at the stove. "Ward," he reminded her. "I make dinner every evening, so this is no trouble at all, Reyna. I've got to keep that boy fed."

"The boy" to which he referred was Ben, and he would be home soon. He'd insisted Reyna drive his truck back here while he waited for the repairs to her vehicle. He'd be along shortly, he'd insisted. That had been an hour ago. The flat tire hadn't been such a big deal, but there had been damage to some steering component that needed to be repaired. The mechanic had assured Reyna he could do it, but it would take a little time. Ben had wanted to hang around and supervise the work.

"I appreciate being invited to dinner," Reyna said.

"Did you have a productive day?"

She supposed that was his way of asking if she'd learned anything. "Ben showed me around the Henry place. We had lunch at the diner, where I met Mr. and Mrs. McGill."

"She's a sight," he pointed out. "Still believes my son duped her younger brother."

"She mentioned something about that." Reyna opted to see what Ward had to say before offering what Vinnia McGill had insinuated.

"Vinnia always has plenty to say about folks. Most of it's slanted to suit the point she hopes to make."

Reyna had definitely gotten that impression.

"JR had no idea Lucinda had agreed to marry Gordon when they started seeing each other. She lied to him. Lied to them both."

"I suppose there was quite the backlash when Walls came back and found out what she'd done."

"Not so much," Ward said as he scooped soup into a bowl. "If he'd made too much of it, he would only have looked like the loser. As I recall, he played it off like he was grateful to be rid of her."

Vinnia certainly hadn't appeared to think so.

"Wounds unattended have a tendency to fester," Reyna offered. "Especially as time goes by with nothing left to do but look at it."

Gordon Walls had remained in the Whispering Winds community. He'd had to watch the woman who was supposed to marry him grow round with another man's child… marry that other man and build a home together.

Ward placed a steaming bowl of soup on the table in front of her. Then loaded one for himself. "I can't argue with your reasoning," he said as he took a seat at the table with her. "But I can tell you that me and Jacob Evans pretty much ruled out Gordon's involvement in whatever happened to our boys."

"Jacob Evans?" Then she remembered that was Judson Evans's father's name.

"Judson's daddy. A few days after they disappeared, he and I picked up Gordon and had a little talk with him."

Reyna could just imagine how that had gone down. "Dare I ask how that played out?"

He eyed her for a long moment. "I'm certain you've seen enough movies to know when a man believes someone has hurt someone he cares about, things can get ugly."

Reyna nodded. "You might want to refrain from filling in the details."

He chuckled. "The end result was that Jacob and I were both convinced that Gordon had nothing to do with what happened to our boys."

Reyna picked up her spoon and took a bite of the soup. "Mmm. This really is delicious."

"It was my mother's favorite soup. Whenever times got tight, we lived on this soup."

The perfect opening for moving into another territory she'd wanted to explore. "Did any of the Three or their families have any particular financial issues during the time of the disappearance?"

"Everyone has trouble now and then. Some more than others." He shrugged. "But there was nothing out of the ordinary, to my knowledge. If the other families had any troubles—financial or otherwise—they kept them quiet."

Reyna ate for a while. Couldn't resist. She felt guilty for not waiting for Ben, but he'd insisted she shouldn't.

Eventually, she resumed her questioning. "Was there anything going on with JR or the others that had you concerned? Any sort of restlessness or dissatisfaction?"

"Lucinda was all torn up about JR quitting his job in the city. Duke Fuller had been talking about selling everything and moving to Nashville—even though he'd promised to fix up the Henry place for his wife. Judson Evans was pitching some new venture to his daddy. That boy never had to worry about a job. His daddy would always take care of him. I suppose those things fall into one or both of those categories."

Reyna agreed. She supposed that was what Father Cullen had been referring to. "The official investigation looked into the possibility of a kidnapping gone wrong."

He nodded, pushed away his empty bowl. "Never was a ransom demand. Truth is one investigation or the other looked into most every possibility of what could have happened. But it didn't bring them any closer to figuring it out."

"Based on the things you mentioned were happening, did you ever feel as if the guys were on the verge of something?"

"They were young. One or the other was always on the verge of something, but what's new? It's the sort of thing that drives treasure hunters and scientists alike."

Reyna hesitated a moment. She wanted to go for shocking, but she felt guilty doing so with Ward. Still, he wanted the truth. She wanted it. Why not just do it? "If you had to choose one of the Three," she said, "who was capable of killing the other two, which one would it be?"

The shock and anger she'd expected to see didn't come. Instead, he gazed steadily at her. "If I had to choose," he repeated, "I would say Duke for sure. He was older and more hotheaded. But—" he stared directly at Reyna "—I would bet my life that whatever happened was not prompted or carried out by one of those boys."

Reyna didn't remind him that they had been men—grown men—at the time of the disappearance. She understood that he was speaking as a father who would forever see his son as his boy.

If none of the three men had precipitated the event somehow, had it been one of their wives? Or one of the parents?

"There's plenty more," he said, gesturing to her empty bowl.

"I'm good, thank you. It was wonderful." Reyna studied the man who took their empty bowls to the sink. Who had wanted to hurt the Three or wanted to get rid of them badly enough to actually make it happen?

Ben arrived, and his grandfather insisted he join Reyna at the table while he ladled up his dinner.

Ben passed her keys to her. "Everything's taken care of."

"Thanks. I'm really glad there wasn't more damage."

He nodded, flashed a smile for his grandfather as he settled a bowl of soup on the table in front of him and produced a glass of iced tea.

Ben was clearly starving. Reyna occupied herself with tracing a bead of sweat down her own tea glass while he ate.

She thought of the parents of the Three who were still living. JR's mother had passed away. Duke Fuller's father had died, but his mother was still alive. Both Judson Evans's parents had passed. As awful as it was to think of a parent harming an offspring, it happened. But the age group of the men when they'd disappeared put the possibility lower on the probability scale.

"Thanks, Pops—that was great." Ben pushed aside his bowl and settled his attention on Rey. "Have you ever had any trouble with that tire?"

The question surprised her. "No. I mean, the Land Rover is old, so there are mechanical issues from time to time, but the tires are fairly new."

"No slow air leaks? No previous repairs?"

She shook her head. "Was the tire defective?"

"The best we could determine, the tire was cut, punctured in a way that prevented the air from seeping out until the vehicle was moving, and then it came out quickly. You're lucky it wasn't a rear tire, or you might have lost complete control of the vehicle. With a front tire, you still have some control with the steering wheel. Not so with a rear blowout."

Reyna drew back as if needing distance from the words he'd uttered. "You're saying you believe someone did this on purpose." It wasn't a question. Of course—that was what he'd said. But...why? How?

"Yes. I'm saying someone did this and it was on purpose—no question."

The idea was ludicrous. "It had to have happened while I was at the church. I went to Nelson Owens's house first, but we were on the porch the whole time with my vehicle in clear view. Then I drove to the church, and I was there maybe forty-five minutes. An hour, tops." This was crazy…and yet her nerves were suddenly jangling.

"Did anyone know you were going to the church?"

Reyna thought about the question. "Eudora, of course. I don't think I mentioned where I was going next to Owens." Not that she could see either one having anything to do with her tire being damaged.

This was too much.

"Maybe," Ben said, "going off on your own while you're conducting these interviews isn't such a good idea."

"This is the way I've always conducted interviews and done my research." How else was she supposed to do it? This was…disturbing. She felt violated.

"I'd feel a lot better if you would let me tag along."

Was he serious? "Don't you have work to do?"

"Nothing that won't wait."

Again, this made no sense.

"Why would you even want to do this? This tagging-along thing?" It wasn't that she was opposed to company, but—as unkind as it sounded—she needed to be clear on his motive.

He held her gaze for a moment before answering. "My father and his two best friends went missing thirty years ago. Since that time, no less than two dozen people—some official, some not—have looked into their disappearance, and no one has ever found a damned thing."

She nodded. “What does that have to do with your playing the part of my shadow?”

“In all that time, I’ve never heard about any of the folks doing the investigating receiving any sort of threats or being vandalized.”

His words suddenly made way too much sense.

“This tells me,” he went on before she could say anything, “someone is worried you might actually be the one to find what no one else has.”

Chapter Six

Kane Residence
Thistle Lane
Tuesday, April 23, 10:00 a.m.

Ben stood at the kitchen window, staring out over the orchard. As a kid, he'd loved running through those trees and climbing them. Despite his father disappearing when he'd been seven, he'd had a good childhood. He'd had his grandfather and his mother had been there for him. She'd been different then. Always smiling and laughing. Always baking cookies and thinking up games to play. She'd seen that he'd had all the things a kid needed. He'd never once gone without food or clothing or the usual things kids thought were necessary.

But after the disappearance something had been missing—besides his dad. Never with his grandfather, but with his mother. There had been a distance. He hadn't recognized it in the earlier days of his youth, but as he'd grown into a teenager, it had become more and more clear. At the time he'd assumed it was the usual teenage angst that had created a gulf. But in more recent years, rather than see that gap close, it had somehow become wider.

For a long while he'd ignored it as nothing more than his

mother's way, but he saw it differently now. He'd gone through the possibilities. Maybe she was depressed. Sad. Lonely. But then he'd slowly realized it was something else. She was hiding something. The biggest visible change had started five years ago when a Chattanooga reporter had decided to do a twenty-fifth anniversary special about the Three. The dynamics between him and his mother had changed dramatically. Her connection with the other Widows—all the relationships he was aware of—had shifted.

He'd told himself that people changed when they got older. She'd been fifty-three at the time. Maybe she'd experienced a later-life crisis. Anytime he'd brought up the subject, she had bristled. Eventually she'd lowered the boom, letting him know that his questions were not appreciated and would no longer be tolerated.

"She's here."

Ben turned at the sound of his mother's voice. Instead of responding to her less-than-enthusiastic announcement, he said, "I was just remembering how I loved to climb in all those apple trees. Dad used to boost me up when I was really little."

She didn't smile. "I remember when you fell out and broke your arm."

That was Lucinda Kane. Always recalling the downside of the past.

By the time Reyna had climbed the steps and was just about to knock on the front door, he was there and opened it. Her fist hesitated in the air, then dropped to her side.

"Good morning," she said.

"Morning." Time would tell if it was a good one. "Come on in."

Reyna stepped inside and looked around, her gaze lingering on the family photos on the walls.

Ben closed the door and watched for a while as she walked toward one photograph in particular. It was the largest of the framed images. The last one taken before his father had vanished. Ben had just turned seven. The photo had been shot at his grandfather's home, down by the barn beneath Ben's favorite tree.

He didn't rush her, just let her look her fill. His mother would be waiting in the parlor, braced and ready for battle. The whole idea made no sense. Why couldn't she be glad that someone was trying to find the truth? Someone, he'd decided, who was in it for more than some misplaced hope of notoriety.

Someone who, apparently, just by showing up had disturbed the thirty-year-old cloak of silence that surrounded the disappearance.

"How was your night?" he asked when her interest shifted from the photographs to him.

She smiled. He liked her smile. He gave himself a mental shake. What he really needed was to get out more.

"Thankfully uneventful. Birdie showed me dozens of photo albums. Vintage photos of the town and the folks who live here." Reyna gave a nod. "I'm reasonably confident I know most of your secrets now."

If Birdie Jewel was doing the talking, Ben would bet Reyna knew plenty for sure.

"Let's head into the parlor. My mom's waiting there."

Lucinda Kane stood in front of the pink chair that had been her favorite for as long as Ben could remember. Each time the fabric grew worn, she had it recovered. She always insisted there was something to be said for good furniture.

"Mom, this is Reyna Hart," he announced when she at last looked up and acknowledged their presence. Deep down he hoped her reasons for always being so stubborn about this subject were genuine and not because she was hiding some secret he really didn't want to learn.

Reyna approached his mother, extended her hand. "It's a pleasure to meet you, Ms. Kane. I appreciate your time."

His mother reached out and grasped Reyna's hand ever so briefly before drawing away. "I'm certain my son told you that I'm only doing this to appease him."

"He did," Reyna said. "This is a difficult subject for you, so I can understand your hesitation."

Lucinda gestured to the sofa. "Please, sit. Ben, would you get our guest coffee or water?"

"Not necessary," Reyna hastened to say. "I filled up on coffee at breakfast. Birdie makes the best coffee."

"I'm sure you're finding her B and B welcoming." Lucinda settled into her chair.

"I am," Reyna confirmed. "She's an interesting lady—well versed in the history of Whispering Winds. She's had me enthralled since I arrived."

His mother cocked her head and eyed Reyna for a moment. "You can't always believe everything you hear, Ms. Hart, not even from Birdie Jewel."

Reyna smiled. "We all have our own way of remembering," she agreed. "We tell our memories from our own perspective, so what might feel like an error or oversight is more often simply the way a person remembers."

Ben looked from his mother to Reyna. "Interesting way of seeing things."

Frankly, he'd never thought of it that way, but it made sense. Maybe this was the problem with his and his mother's way of seeing the past. Definitely something to consider.

"My son says you have questions for me," Lucinda said, clearly ready to move on.

"I think we should just rip the Band-Aid off and start with the hard questions first," Reyna suggested.

Ben braced for his mother's rebuttal.

"Very well," she said instead.

Surprised but grateful, he relaxed marginally.

"Why did you change your mind about wanting to marry Gordon Walls?"

Even Ben was a little put off by the question. His attention swung to his mother, expecting to see anger and shock. Instead he saw a face clean of emotion and intently focused on the woman asking the questions.

"I was young. Gordon had all these big plans for getting out of Whispering Winds, and I wanted that very much. His Army uniform was impressive. It seemed like the perfect plan for getting away. I imagined traveling the world with him in the military." She sighed. "I was just a foolish girl with silly dreams."

Never once had he heard this version of his mother's decision. Strangely, it made a great deal of sense.

"But then you met JR," Reyna went on. "You knew him before, I'm guessing."

"We both grew up right here in Whispering Winds, so of course I knew him. But he'd just come back from college, and…he'd changed. Matured. He was very different from Gordon. Far more handsome, but also kinder, more deeply passionate about everything. As they say, he swept me off my feet."

"How did Gordon react to this?" Reyna asked the next logical question.

Ben held his breath. This was the aspect of her history that his mother most often refused to speak about.

"I think he was relieved."

Ben did a double take. Had she really just said that to basically a stranger?

"He put up a bit of a fuss to save face, but I personally believe he already had other plans and my decision gave him the out he needed."

"Why have you never said that before?" The question was out before Ben could tamp it back.

Lucinda smiled in his direction. "Because it was embarrassing. I didn't want to admit that Gordon had likely outgrown his brief infatuation with me." She sent him a pointed look. "Why don't you find those family photo albums from back then and show them to Reyna? She might find them interesting."

"I'd love to see them," Reyna agreed.

Ben pushed to his feet, his brain wobbling with disbelief. Who was this impostor, and where was his mother?

Evans Residence
Blackberry Trail
12:25 p.m.

DEIDRE FULLER HAD refused to meet with Reyna. She wasn't so surprised. Frankly, she'd been shocked that Ben's mom and now Ms. Evans had agreed to an interview. Ben, on the other hand, seemed completely surprised by Fuller's decision.

He parked his truck next to Rey's Land Rover. When he opened his door to get out, she did the same. The Evans home was typical of the area and not unlike the homes of the other two widows: farmhouse, two stories, well maintained. There were many houses of this style in the area, but what continued to amaze Reyna was the idea that these women had lived in the same ones for all these years. None had ever remarried, and none had sold the homes purchased by their husbands. Reyna would have thought that at least one of the Widows would have moved on by now, particularly since two had no children with the spouses who had disappeared.

Why stay in that same place with the same memories and no forward momentum during all this time?

On top of all that, the houses were very short distances apart. They were all on different roads on the fringes of Whispering Winds, but they were only a mile or so from each other.

"I enjoyed meeting your mother," Reyna said as she and Ben climbed the steps to the front porch. "The photo albums provided such a great sense of time and place for my research."

"Mother startled even me with her cooperativeness," he confessed. "I expected each answer to be like pulling teeth."

Reyna laughed. "Sometimes those closest to us surprise us the most." She wondered if he understood how lucky he was to still have his mother and his grandfather. She had no one left but her mother. As much as she loved her mom, she dearly missed her grandmother.

At the door of the Evans home, Ben hesitated. "I think we should have dinner together again so you can share your insights from the day."

She nodded. "I think we can work that out."

This research trip continued to throw her curveballs. She hadn't expected to have her tire vandalized, and she certainly hadn't anticipated being welcomed so wholeheartedly by one of the families she needed to investigate. Mostly, the unexpected attentiveness of this man astonished her.

As he knocked on the door, she reminded herself that this might very well be nothing more than his determination to know her every step. To be involved with how she conducted her research.

For now, she opted to believe his intentions were sincere and that there were no ulterior motives.

The door opened, and Harlowe Evans stood in the entryway. Younger than the other widows by only a couple of months, Evans kept her hair the same blond shade it had been in her youth. Her makeup was flawless, as was her spring attire—khaki trousers and a floral shirt with just the right hint of blue to highlight her eyes.

"Ben." She drew back. "Come in." Her attention fixed on Reyna as the two stepped inside. "Ms. Hart, such a pleasure to meet you. I read your book!" Her eyes twinkled. "*The Woman at the End of the Lane.* It was wonderful!"

"Thank you." Reyna couldn't help feeling a burst of pride when anyone mentioned having read her book. She doubted she would ever get past the blush that right this second heated her cheeks and the little stream of excitement that zipped through her. She suspected that feeling would never get old if she published a hundred novels.

"I have a little something prepared for lunch," Evans said, "if you're interested."

Ben patted his stomach. "Sounds good to me, Ms. Evans. I can always eat."

The older woman made a happy face. "Well, come on, then."

They followed her to the kitchen. This farmhouse had been gutted at some point, Reyna decided. Most of the first floor was a huge open space. Very different from the others. She wondered if the open floor plan happened before or after the disappearance. Not that it really mattered, but it would be interesting to know if Evans was the only one of the Widows who had moved forward in any manner.

On the massive island that stood between the kitchen and main living area Reyna spotted neatly halved sandwiches and other finger foods as well as a sweating pitcher of lemonade, judging by the sheer number of lemons floating in the otherwise clear liquid.

"We have my fave cucumber sandwiches and those ham-and-cheese ones I know you like, Ben." She looked to Reyna. "We can munch while you ask questions. I'll pour the drinks—you two grab a plate and fill it up."

While Reyna picked through the yummy-looking offerings, she asked, "You, Lucinda and Deidre have been best friends your whole lives, is that right?"

"It is," Evans said as she slid onto a stool and surveyed her plate. She went for a cucumber sandwich. "We knew each other in church, of course, and then we started kindergarten together. We were always inseparable."

Reyna had decided to approach this interview from a different perspective. "I'm sure the three of you struggled with the usual teenage issues."

Who hadn't?

Evans chewed for a moment, then swallowed. "Not so much. There were a few times we stopped speaking to each other but never for more than a day. We've always been extremely close."

"Getting married didn't change this?" Reyna nibbled a cucumber sandwich and hummed her satisfaction. "So good."

"Why, thank you." Evans gave a nod. "Now, to answer your question, I think we got a lot closer after we married."

She smiled at Ben. "When your mama had you it was like we all had you. So exciting and so scary at the same time."

Ben grinned. "My mom says you two spoiled me."

"We did," Evans agreed.

"Do you mind sharing why you never had children?" Reyna asked, steeling herself for a backlash. It was not the most polite of questions.

"I don't know if you've spoken with Deidre already, but she'll tell you that she never wanted children. As much as she enjoyed being a part of Ben's life, she didn't have any desire to go there personally."

Reyna chose not to mention that Fuller had passed on the interview.

"I, on the other hand, would have loved to have babies." She smiled sadly. "Unfortunately, my Judson had issues in that area." She leaned toward Reyna and whispered, "Low sperm count." Then she straightened. "I never wanted to make him feel pressured, and back then it was not so easy to do the things you can do now. Then he was gone, and I just let it go."

Felt like the perfect segue to another important question. "I find it curious that none of you have remarried or even moved from Whispering Winds. Have you discussed this between the three of you?"

Evans took a moment, drank some lemonade, picked at the food left on her plate. Then she met Reyna's gaze. "We were never going to talk about this, but—" she looked from Reyna to Ben and back "—I guess it's time we did."

Her comment had other questions jumping in Reyna's head, but she kept quiet for fear of causing Evans to change her mind about whatever she intended to say.

"After...what happened, we made a vow that we would not even look at anyone else or consider moving on with our lives until we had answers..." She exhaled a sad sound. "We really did expect them to come back. I mean, how do three men just vanish? It felt like a dream—a nightmare. We kept expecting to wake up and find everything the way it was before."

Except that had never happened.

"As the years passed, did you revisit this decision?" Reyna held her breath, hoping she would continue to answer the questions no one else had so far.

"We did once or twice. But no one wanted to say the words—that they were never coming back. It was easier to believe they'd come walking through those doors just anytime."

She stared at her front door as she said this.

Her words and her voice were so sincere. Reyna found it difficult to believe she wasn't being honest. But it felt like such a stretch. Who waited thirty years for a man to return?

"When was the last time the three of you discussed what happened?" Reyna asked.

Evans frowned. She blinked, once, twice. "Well, it's been a while. We're all busy, and life just kind of slips by."

Now she was evading. The change was easy to see and hear.

"With the three of you still being so close," Reyna said, redirecting, "I imagine you talk of those hard days fairly often."

The deer-caught-in-the-headlights expression was impossible to ignore. "Not as much as you'd think."

Another evasion.

"But you are still very close," Reyna suggested.

Slow, vague nod. "Like sisters." She picked up a cheese straw and poked it into her mouth.

"That's so unusual," Reyna pointed out, hoping to shift the tension. "I've lost touch with everyone I knew in school."

Evans only nodded.

Reyna had a feeling the interview was over.

Ben pulled his cell phone from his pocket and checked the screen. "Excuse me—I need to take this."

He stepped away from the table.

She decided to try one more avenue. "I love the open floor plan you've created in your house. It's really lovely."

Evans looked around as if she wasn't sure what Reyna meant. "It works."

Ben reappeared. "We have to go," he said to Reyna.

The worry on his face had her moving off the stool. "Everything okay?"

Rather than answer her, he said, "Thanks so much, Ms. Evans. We may call you again, if that's okay."

Reyna pulled a card from her bag and passed it to the woman. "Call me if you think of anything that might help."

"Absolutely," Evans insisted, her tone and expression back to open and sincere. "Y'all come back anytime."

They were outside and moving toward their parked vehicles before he explained: "Pops called. There's been a fire at the B and B."

Reyna's heart hit the ground. "Is Birdie okay?" As far as Reyna knew, there were no other guests… This was just terrible.

"Don't know. We need to get over there now."

Chapter Seven

The Jewel Bed & Breakfast
Main Street
2:15 p.m.

The small Whispering Winds fire department had deployed both their fire engine and their fire truck. Thankfully no one had needed rescuing. Birdie had smelled the smoke, discovered the flames and made the call as she'd hurried out of the building.

With the fire department just down the road, the trucks had arrived in mere moments. The flames had been extinguished, and the building had been cleared.

Birdie sat on a bench in the front gardens, staring tearfully at her beloved bed-and-breakfast.

"I'm so glad you're okay." Reyna sat down beside her. She didn't even want to consider how things could have gone. Fires in old buildings were particularly ravenous. The older structures hadn't been built with the more modern deterrents. Not to mention the sheer age of the wood made it highly flammable.

Birdie worked up a smile. "My insurance agent insisted I install those smoke detectors years ago." She shook her head, swiped at a tear that had slipped past her hold on her emotions. "I'm so very glad I did."

Reyna looped her arm around the woman's shoulders and gave her a hug. "Me too."

Birdie turned to her then. "How's your research going? I've been hearing all sorts of rumbles from the natives." She smiled. "Everyone knows there's a stranger in town digging around in the most painful part of our past."

Reyna supposed she couldn't deny the description. "Progress is slow. I was able to interview two of the Widows—Lucinda Kane and Harlowe Evans. Deidre Fuller refuses to see me."

Birdie sighed. "Deidre was always a bit full of herself. The truth is she always wanted to give the perception of utter grace and wealth. You know the sort. Dory and I used to shake our heads at how some folks thought they had to prove they were above the rest of us."

"Dory?" Reyna suspected she meant Eudora, but she had never heard about any nickname from the lady.

She looked away. "Eudora. That was my nickname for her. We've known each other our whole lives."

Reyna felt guilty for being here two days already without another call to Eudora to update her. She'd have to call her tonight. She would be very interested in learning that Reyna had spoken at length with two of the three Widows. If she was feeling particularly lucid, she might even have some insights into how to prod Deidre Fuller into talking. It never hurt to ask.

"I'll tell her you said hello," Reyna promised. "I plan to call her tonight and catch up."

Birdie's smile widened, reached her blue eyes. "That would be very nice. Thank you."

Reyna studied the beautiful old mansion that had been lovingly transformed into a bed-and-breakfast. Birdie had done much of the work herself, and the gardens she had created were nothing short of spectacular. "Have they given you any sense of the damage inside?"

"I only know that the trouble was on the second floor."

Reyna's room was on the second floor. Her laptop was in the room. And her clothes. Nothing that couldn't be replaced, of course.

Ben had gone in search of the sheriff. Now there were three Hamilton County sheriff's department vehicles in the street. Reyna knew from her research that a small substation was here on Main Street, and the sheriff, Tara Norwood—the daughter of retired sheriff Tarrence Norwood—was a local from nearby Dread Hollow. Reyna imagined she kept her finger on the pulse of local goings-on.

"Oh my," Birdie said as she grasped Reyna's hand. "I hope your things weren't damaged."

If the laptop was ruined, it wouldn't be so bad. Reyna always saved everything to the cloud. Her notes and videos from Eudora—her work—everything was backed up. She usually typed up a sort of daily report each evening. This technique worked well for her.

"We're not going to worry about that," Reyna assured the older woman. "There's nothing in there that can't be easily replaced."

Birdie released her hand and pressed her own to her chest. "Thank goodness. Back when I was your age, to have the physical pages destroyed would have been the end of my work. Things weren't so easy back then."

Reyna was aware. The days of manually typed manuscripts and notes, with only a copy machine to back up the work, were a little unnerving. The writer's life was certainly simpler today—at least, in terms of saving and transferring one's work.

Ben walking in their direction had Reyna pushing the

thoughts away. She hoped for Birdie's sake that the damage was minimal.

"Is it bad?" Birdie asked, her hands wringing in her lap.

"It could have been much worse." Ben glanced back at the firefighters going in and out of the front entrance of the building. "The fire was contained to only one room." He turned to Reyna. "Yours."

She was pleased to know the damage had been contained to a small area, but that it was her room suddenly seemed odd. "I don't smoke, and I had no candles lit." She frowned. "In fact, I don't think there were even any candles in the room." She looked to Birdie for confirmation.

She shrugged. "None that I'm aware of. I've had guests bring candles and incense, but I've never had one start a fire."

Reyna flinched. "With me away all day, I can't imagine how it started."

"The fire marshal is conducting an investigation," Ben explained. "Sheriff Norwood said you wouldn't be able to rent any more rooms until the investigation is complete and cleanup has been done, Birdie."

She waved the idea off. "Of course. I'm sure the whole place smells like smoke."

He made a face. "Unfortunately."

Reyna drew in a big breath. "I'll need to find a clothing shop." Everything she'd brought with her was now beyond her reach...if it had survived the damage to her room.

Ben hitched a thumb back toward the entrance. "The sheriff said there was one smaller bag in the bathroom and it was okay. She'll bring it out for you."

Her meager cosmetics and underthings. Relief flashed through Reyna. "I would really appreciate that." She glanced down at her jeans and shirt. "I can just wash and wear this over and over." No biggie.

"Certainly you cannot. We can't have you conducting your interviews in the same clothes over and over," Birdie argued. "I have things you can wear. As soon as I'm allowed to go inside, I'll put together a little care package for you."

"Thank you," Reyna said. "That would be helpful."

A woman in a sheriff's uniform approached. "The fire marshal is almost finished," she said, her statement directed at Birdie. "We can go inside and go over everything with you once he's done."

"Thank you so much, Tara," Birdie said. "I just can't believe this happened."

Reyna felt terrible. The idea that the fire had something to do with why she was here made her feel ill.

"Sheriff Norwood," Ben said, "this is Reyna Hart. Her room is the one where the fire started."

Tara gave Reyna a nod. "I'm sure sorry we have to meet under such circumstances, Ms. Hart."

"Reyna," she offered as she pushed to her feet. "I'm just confused about how it started. There didn't appear to be any electrical issues in the room." She'd used her laptop and phone chargers in two of the outlets. The lamps had all worked fine. Oh, and she'd used the hair dryer in the bathroom.

"That's the odd part," Norwood explained. "There was a lit candle in the room, and it apparently fell over."

Reyna drew back as if she'd been slapped. "A candle? But there weren't any candles in the room, and I certainly didn't bring any with me." She shrugged. "I don't have matches or a lighter. Even if there had been a candle, I wouldn't have been able to light it."

Norwood held up her hands, palms out. “My statement wasn’t an accusation. Based on the time you left your room—Birdie said before nine this morning—the candle would have burned out long before now. The fire marshal’s report will give us a more accurate timeline. But I’m guessing it was lit around noon.”

“I had lunch at the diner,” Birdie said. Her mouth rounded for a moment. “I always leave the front entrance unlocked in case a guest returns while I’m away. You know I never go far.”

“I wish you had video cameras,” Norwood said. “Most of the shops along Main have added them in recent years.”

She waved off the idea. “I’m too old to worry with that sort of thing. I’ll leave it to the next owner to bother.”

Norwood smiled patiently. “Let’s go conduct a walk-through, Ms. Birdie.”

She stood, then turned back to Reyna. “I’ll bring you some clothes in just a few minutes.”

“Thank you.”

Reyna watched the two head back to the entrance and disappear inside. Then she turned to face Ben. “Sheriff Norwood didn’t say it, but she has to see that whoever started the fire had targeted me in particular.” She shrugged. “I mean, what else is there to think?”

Ben glanced toward the activity at the bed-and-breakfast. “She believes that’s the case,” he confirmed. “She asked me a lot of questions about who you’d been talking to and that kind of thing.” He moved his head side to side, the gesture slow, worried. “I told her about your tire. I’m getting a bad feeling about all this.”

“So am I.” As unsettling as this was, Reyna would not be scared off. “Is there another motel around here?”

“You’re going home with me,” he said, his gaze settling on hers. "Sheriff Norwood thought it was a good idea as well."

Well, if the sheriff thought it was a good idea, how could she say no?

Kane Residence
Lula Lake Lane
8:30 p.m.

"I DIDN'T MENTION the fire when I spoke to Eudora," Reyna said.

Ben placed the final plate he'd dried in the cabinet. "It would only have upset her." He didn't know the elderly woman well, but he remembered her from when she'd been a schoolteacher. She'd still been teaching at Whispering Winds Elementary when he'd been a kid.

Reyna propped a hip against the counter and smiled. "I could hear the smile in her voice when I talked about Birdie. She misses being here."

He walked to the coffee maker and checked the water level. "You up for a cup of coffee?"

"Coffee would be nice."

"How about you, Pops?" He turned to his grandfather, who still sat at the table. He'd been listening avidly to their conversation about the fire at the bed-and-breakfast and the other events of the day.

"No, thanks." He pushed to his feet. "I think I'll turn in a little early, finish that book I started last week."

"Good night, Ward," Reyna called after him.

"Night, Pops."

Ward waved as he shuffled on out of the kitchen. He seemed more tired lately than usual. Ben hoped this business wasn't taking an extra toll on him. As much as his grandfather wanted to find the truth, was it really worth it at this point?

"You're worried this is too much for him," Reyna offered.

Ben went back to the business of making coffee. "Yeah. It's a lot to deal with."

"For you as well," she pointed out.

He pressed the start button on the machine and listened for the sounds that indicated it was beginning the brew process. Then he turned to his guest. "Not as much as for him." He reached into the cabinet for a couple of coffee mugs. "We're kind of programmed for losing parents." He set the mugs on the counter. Shrugged. "Maybe not at seven years old, but the concept is a part of growing up. But losing a child…" He shook his head. "No one is ever prepared for that."

"Valid point," she agreed. "I hadn't stopped to consider that even though your father was twenty-eight, he was still Ward's child—his only child."

The scent of coffee filled the room in the silence that followed. Ben waded through the years, searching for memories of his father. "I don't remember a lot about him. Pops tried to keep his memories alive for me. But Mom…" He shrugged again. "She turned it all off a few months after the disappearance. It was like she understood what had happened, had accepted it and wanted to move on. I resented her for a long time because of that."

Reyna searched his face, looking for the emotions behind his words. He didn't really want her to see them.

He hadn't actually meant to share quite so much, but there was something about the way Sheriff Norwood had watched him, scrutinized his every word today when they'd been surveying Reyna's room. The sheriff thought something was going on related to the Three as well. She hadn't gone out on a limb and said as much, but Ben sensed she'd been seeing it and trying to make sense of it.

Thirty years was a long time for someone to protect a secret.

In all this time with the dozens of investigators and reporters who had poked around in the case, there had never been this sort of trouble or backlash. Why now? Why with Reyna Hart?

What was it about her or how she was going about her research that made someone nervous?

Once the coffee had brewed and mugs had been filled, they moved to the parlor. The quiet down the hall nudged Ben again. He should check on his grandfather. But then he'd only complain. Ward Kane did not like to be treated as if he were helpless or needy.

"Do you mind if I browse through the family photo albums again?"

He exiled the troubling thoughts about his grandfather. "I do not." He settled his mug on the table by the sofa and helped Reyna round up the many photo albums his grandfather had ensured remained safe through the years. Then they sat side by side on the sofa.

"My grandmother was the one who always made sure there were family photos of all the important events—holidays, birthdays and stuff like that. After she was gone, Pops took over and did a pretty good job."

"What about your mother? Her albums seemed thorough as well."

"Mostly. Sometimes Pops would make extra copies of photos he'd taken for her. Her documentation was more thorough before the disappearance."

Reyna turned a page in the older of the albums that included Ben as an infant.

"She seemed happy." She tapped a photo of Ben and his parents. He couldn't have been more than a few months old.

"Pops says they were happy." When Ben had gotten older he'd asked his mother about his father and whether they'd been happy, and she had usually changed the subject. Eventually he'd stopped asking. It was easier to believe what he wanted and to take his grandfather's word for how things were.

"Was this at your grandmother's funeral?"

Ben studied the photo and nodded. "Yeah." He tapped the Victorian-style house in the background. "You probably saw this place when you were driving through town. Addison Funeral Home. It's been here forever. They were one of the first funeral homes in the area to have their own crematorium." He laughed. "But no one wanted to use it. It was a long time before folks around here even considered going that route with a deceased loved one. But the Addisons liked being ahead of the times. They're one of the few funeral homes that hasn't sold out to a chain. Pops says you can do that when the family is independently wealthy."

Reyna smiled. "I like hearing stories from the past. It helps put life back then in perspective," she said, her attention back on the photos. "Your family seemed happy before the disappearance. You never sensed any issues?"

"Never." He shrugged. "But I was a kid. Kids don't always notice."

Reyna set the album aside. "But other people do, and everyone I've interviewed says the same," she began. "Eudora said the Three were happy, had beautiful wives and good lives. She always says it doesn't make sense that they just vanished. Birdie said almost the same thing. Your grandfather. There has been no one except Vinnia McGill who believes that things weren't storybook."

He saw where she was going now. "You planning to attempt an interview with Gordon Walls?"

"I think I need to," she said. "His role in your mother's life was a major one. Pretending that didn't happen or didn't alter attitudes and perceptions is just too much of a reach."

Yeah, he got that.

"Her relationship with Walls has always been downplayed or left out of the story," he offered, "whenever anyone talks about the Three and what happened."

She nodded. "I just find that odd, but maybe it's because I'm an outsider. They all knew one another. It's possible the idea is as nonsensical to those who know Walls as the opposite is to me."

"I guess so. I've never been around him that much. I've seen his name in the news when he's made major arrests, but that's about it." Ben thought about what he wanted to say next. "I feel like my grandfather would have been the first to go after him if he'd believed he might be involved somehow."

"He mentioned that he and Jacob Evans had a talk with Walls and felt comfortable that he wasn't involved. Still, I would be interested in hearing Walls's side of the story."

"He never told me that," Ben confessed. "Makes sense though. Pops wouldn't have played it off. He would have gone straight in and found out for himself."

"He didn't give me the details," Reyna explained. "Only that he was confident in the answer he got."

He imagined his grandfather thirty years ago kicking

the guy's butt and demanding answers. Not the sort of thing you told your grandson, he supposed.

She continued poring through photos, and the conversation lapsed.

Ben finished off his coffee and relaxed into the sofa. He hadn't gotten one thing done on the Henry place today. In fact, he hadn't gotten any work done at all, and still he was tired. But not too tired to continue talking to Reyna. Maybe he'd been out of the dating game so long he'd forgotten how good it was to have someone his own age—a woman, at that—to just talk with.

"Do you mind if I ask a personal question?" He decided turnabout was fair play. At least, he hoped so.

She put the latest album she'd been perusing aside and picked up her mug. "After the way I've been digging around in your life, how could I ever say no?"

"Why only one book?" He smiled. "I mean, it's only been five years, and maybe you have one in the pipeline as we speak. But I checked your website and your publisher's website. I didn't see anything coming up."

"There's a very good reason for that." She laughed softly, placed her empty mug on the coffee table next to his. "There is no second book. Not so far, anyway."

She sat back, curled her bare feet beneath her. He liked that she felt comfortable enough to do that despite the obviously uncomfortable question he'd asked.

"Sales were actually pretty good, but my publisher wasn't interested in another book—at least, not the ideas for the ones I offered." She was quiet for a moment before going on. "That sort of thing happens more often than you'd think, so I figured the best thing to do was just go on with my life and not consider my brief career as a published author a total failure."

Now he really did feel like a chump for asking.

"These memory books you write," he said, hoping to make up for bringing the subject into the conversation. "It sounds like the families really appreciate your work. It's an amazing thing you do for your clients."

"I enjoy the work, and I do feel it's an important service to my clients as well as their families." She turned her hands up. "I have to say being here and researching this long-ago mystery is making me yearn to dive into fiction again. Maybe something based on a true event."

"Like this one," he countered.

"I'm not so sure that would be appropriate. This is Eudora's memory. Whatever happens with this one, it's for her." Her gaze connected with his. "And maybe for the families involved."

A horn blowing sounded outside.

What the hell? Ben stood and walked toward the front window. The continuous sound was more like someone had laid down on a horn and not let up. There were no other vehicles outside. His truck, his grandfather's and Rey's Land Rover. But his was the one with the horn blowing—the flashing headlights confirmed as much.

"Is something wrong?" Reyna stood beside him now.

"The alarm on my truck went off." He sent her a pointed look. "Stay put, and I'll have a look."

He went to the front hall and grabbed his truck fob off the table they used for a catchall when it came to keys and hats. When he reached for the door, Reyna was next to him again.

"Never tell a woman to stay put," she warned.

"At least stay behind me."

She didn't argue with that one. He surveyed the porch before stepping across the threshold. As he crossed the porch, he scanned left to right and back. No movement as far as he could see. Since the porch lights only extended to where the vehicles were parked, it was quite dark beyond that point.

He clicked the fob—the horn died and the lights stopped flashing. Still no sign of movement. No other sound.

The breeze kicked up, and something on his windshield flopped. It was tucked down into the slot where the wipers sat in the resting position. Still watching for trouble, Ben reached into the shallow valley and pulled what was a single sheet of paper from beneath one of the wipers.

Three words were written in bold red letters on the plain white piece of paper.

MAKE HER GO.

Chapter Eight

Whispering Winds Sheriff's Department Substation
Main Street
Wednesday, April 24, 10:00 a.m.

Ben parked and shut off the engine. He'd suggested they ride together as a means of ensuring that Reyna stayed safe. Made sense, she supposed, since they were doing the rest of her research together.

Then came the call from the sheriff wanting a meeting with them both.

On the way over to the substation, they had talked about why Sheriff Norwood would want to see them this morning. Obviously it was about the fire or Reyna's research into the Three. But there was a third option and Reyna had hesitated to bring it up, but they were out of time now.

The sheriff was inside waiting for them.

"Do you think Gordon Walls found out I've been asking questions about him?" Reyna had assumed he wouldn't be happy about her delving into the past—his in particular. The same could likely be said of anyone involved, she supposed. Eudora had said there would be those who wouldn't be happy.

Last night's message coupled with the fire and Reyna's damaged tire were fairly solid proof that someone wasn't keen on her being here.

There were plenty of good reasons for that attitude. Reyna understood. Some folks just wanted peace. Others wanted to just keep moving ahead and not look back.

But all things considered, she had to wonder if this was about peace or about protection of secrets.

No matter that she hadn't been here very long—anyone could see there were several folks who might have reason to want to protect their secrets.

Ben glanced toward the substation. "I'm certain he knows. News travels fast in small towns, Reyna. No matter how nice and how pretty you are, folks are curious, and they're going to talk."

Reyna smiled, bit her lip. "I think I should say thank-you."

"Just stating the facts." He reached for his door. "People like keeping their secrets and twisting things around to get their way, but I've never been that kind of guy. I prefer going straight for the truth."

Her smile widened. "Good. I prefer the truth."

It was cooler this morning. She was thankful for Birdie's sweatshirt. The flowers on the front were springy. Reyna had tucked her hair into a ponytail. If she was going to be casual, she might as well go all the way. Her partner in crime wore jeans as well. A button-down shirt in blue that matched his eyes and a vest—the kind workingmen wore—completed the look, which was sharp. He looked nice. Very nice.

She dismissed the thoughts and focused forward.

Inside the substation there was a small lobby. *Small* might've been an overstatement. There was a bulletin board and one chair standing beneath it. The only other door besides the one they'd entered opened, and Sheriff Tara Norwood looked from Ben to Reyna.

"Thanks for coming in. Come on back here. Deputy Travers lent me his office."

They followed her down a short corridor, past a couple of other doors and into an office not much larger than the lobby. There was a desk with a chair behind it and two in front. Norwood took the one behind the desk. Ben waited to sit until Reyna had taken a seat.

"I'm going to get straight to the point," Norwood said. "I'm a little worried about what's happening around here. Generally, I'd leave this little community to the two capable deputies assigned to keep it safe, but this goes way back to my daddy's time as sheriff, so I have a bit of a personal stake."

Reyna was aware that Tara's father, Tarrence, had been sheriff when the Three had disappeared.

"I can assure you, Sheriff," she felt compelled to say, "that I did not come here with the intent to stir up trouble."

"I did a little research on you, Reyna, and I'm confident you did not. Frankly, I'm not sure why these anomalies are happening. We've had all manner of investigators poking around over the years. Never once have we had this sort of reaction from what I can only presume is a local."

Ben reached into his back pocket and pulled out the plastic baggie he'd tucked last night's warning note into. "This was tucked under my windshield last night."

Norwood studied the note. She looked over at Reyna. "You've been here three days and you've received three warnings. I feel like it's time to take this situation more seriously than you may believe is necessary."

"I'm fully aware there's a problem," Reyna countered.

"It's my hope that you won't see my presence as an issue for the community." She mentally crossed her fingers. "I feel like I'm onto something here, and I don't want to let it go."

"It's a free country, Reyna," Norwood assured her. "I'm not suggesting that you can't be here doing exactly what you're doing. To my knowledge, you've broken no laws. You have as much right to be here as anyone. All that said, you are in my county and that makes me ultimately responsible for your safety."

"I'm not letting her out of my sight." Ben spoke up. "She's my grandfather's guest, and I feel responsible for her immediate safety."

"I'm glad to hear it," Norwood said. "You two stick together, and I'll be satisfied for now. Anything new happens, I want to hear about it first. Like I said, this was my daddy's case thirty years ago, and whatever's going on now, I want to ensure that it's handled properly."

"Yes, ma'am," Ben said. "You'll be the first to know if anything else happens or if we find anything that will help with the answers we all want."

"I'm sure this is a little difficult for you, Ben."

"More for my grandfather than me," he countered. "At his age, he's just hoping to finally have some answers before..."

Norwood nodded. "I understand." She rose from her chair. "I should get on to my own office."

Ben stood; Reyna did the same.

"Thank you, Sheriff Norwood." Reyna extended her hand across the desk. "I'll really try to keep a low profile."

Norwood laughed. "In this town I don't think that's possible, Reyna."

Outside, Reyna reminded herself to take in the sunshine and the spring air as she climbed into Ben's truck. So often she forgot to fully appreciate the things in everyday life around her. Nearly every one of her memory clients had said in one way or another that their biggest regret was not taking more time to notice the little things.

Norwood's SUV bumped out onto the street and headed in the direction of Chattanooga. Reyna liked Norwood. Her reputation as a sheriff was excellent, and she seemed to really care about the community. But like everyone else related in any way to this case, she wanted answers and was keeping her finger on the pulse of what Reyna was doing.

Maybe she was right and there was no keeping a low profile when most everyone around you had a reason to watch you. Would she be the one to finally crack the case?

No pressure.

Reyna cleared her head and attempted to focus. She wasn't entirely sure where she and Ben were headed this morning, but he had mentioned going back to the Henry property. She wouldn't mind having a more extended look around there as well.

Just because Deidre Fuller had turned her down on the interview request yesterday didn't mean she wouldn't change her mind today. Reyna intended to try. It never hurt to ask. The worst she could do was say no again.

"Since you've decided to be my shadow and chauffeur," she said to the man who'd just started the engine, "do you mind if we make an unexpected visit to the Fuller residence and see if she'll talk to me?"

He reached for the gearshift. "Why not?"

A rap on Reyna's window made her jump.

Her heart lunged into her throat.

The man standing outside her door wore a deputy's uniform, but the baseball cap and the sunglasses prevented her from recognizing him immediately.

Then she did.

Gordon Walls.

Reyna glanced at Ben.

"Stay put," he warned.

This time she didn't argue with him. He got out and walked around to her side of the vehicle, where Walls waited.

"I need to speak to both of you," Walls said.

Ben glanced at her, and Reyna powered the window down. "I'm listening," she said.

"For the record, I'm more than glad to talk to you if you have questions," Walls said, his tone not exactly angry, more determined. "I'd much prefer that to hearing about you asking other folks questions about me."

"I planned to pay you a visit," she said. "But even so, it never hurts to have other people's perspective on the events that occurred thirty years ago."

Reyna wasn't about to be put off by this man or his uniform.

Walls exhaled a big breath, braced his hands on his hips. "I was not happy about what Lucinda did. That's a fact." He set his shielded gaze on Ben. "But my beef wasn't with your daddy. It was with Lucinda. She's the one who betrayed me. But I got over that before I was even back home. What was the point? She'd found someone new, and I was SOL—if you know what I mean. I moved on. Did it hurt?" He shrugged. "Bruised my ego a bit, but I got over it."

"Maybe," Ben offered, "you can give us your thoughts on what happened to my father and the others."

"You surely read my statement from the original investigation."

"I did," he confirmed.

Reyna had as well. Newly minted Deputy Walls had insisted that he had not seen or spoken with any one of the Three in months when they'd disappeared. Hadn't seen or spoken to Lucinda either.

"Then you know I had nothing to do with what happened."

"But you knew them," Reyna argued. "Knew their habits. Their hangouts."

"The Henry property was the place they were last known to be together before the disappearance," Ben pointed out.

Walls pursed his lips for a second. "They hung out at your granddaddy's barn a lot. That's where I confronted JR. We exchanged a few harsh words. Then I left." He shrugged. "I at least had to make an effort, give people something to say, otherwise they would just make it up."

"Any other places we should check out?" Ben asked. "Over the years, I've been every place anyone has told me about."

Walls weighed the question for a bit. "I remember some talk of those guys having a hangout on the Fuller property out by the lake. During the initial investigation, the property was searched, but nothing was ever found."

"There used to be a cabin out there," Ben said, "but the Fullers said it burned down when Duke was a kid. It no longer existed when they disappeared."

"That's all I can tell you," Walls said. He turned to Reyna. "I hope you'll direct any future questions straight to me."

He walked back to his SUV and climbed in. They watched until he'd exited the parking lot.

Ben suggested, "I say we take a ride out to the Fuller property."

"Should we call her and get permission?" Reyna hoped the answer would be no.

"This is land over by the lake, deep in the woods. I doubt she's been out there in years. She likely won't mind if we have a look."

Reyna fastened her seat belt. "Let's do it."

Trout Lake
11:45 a.m.

BEN HAD FISHED at this lake many times as a kid. First with his father and then with his grandfather. He hadn't been here in years. Truth was he hadn't been fishing in years. He'd spent too much time trying to be the man his ex-fiancée had wanted him to be. As soon as this was over, he was taking his grandfather fishing. Here, the way they'd done when he'd been a kid.

The old gravel driveway was mostly grown over with grass and weeds. He pointed to a leaning stone chimney. "That was the cabin someone in the Fuller family built a few generations back. It burned down right before the disappearance. It had been a long, dry summer. Lightning struck the roof, and it caught fire like dry kindling."

"It's beautiful out here."

Reyna was right. It was one of the most peaceful places on the mountain. Behind the original cabin was dense woods, but when you walked about a mile you hit a clearing that flowed right to the lake. The water was as blue as a cloudless sky, and there was nothing but the sound of nature all around.

"Just wait." He grinned at her. "You ain't seen nothing yet."

She gestured to the No Trespassing signs. "Maybe we should call Ms. Fuller."

"We're following up on a lead," he reminded her. He should call, but he wasn't taking the risk, not after Ms. Fuller had refused to meet with Reyna. What the woman didn't know wouldn't hurt her. They were only having a quick look. Mostly, he was just really tired of the evasive tactics and silence. He wanted answers.

The walk took a few minutes. The underbrush had grown out of hand, but it was worth the trouble. It was clear no one had been out here in years. Definitely no all-terrain or utility vehicles.

When they reached the clearing, Reyna gasped. "Wow."

"Yeah." He watched her take in the scene, her eyes wide with wonder, a smile on her lips. Watching her made his respiration pick up. Or maybe it was the trudge through the thick brush.

The lake was large, and the water was clean and clear. But it was the way it reached toward the cliff side, giving it an infinite edge, that really took your breath.

"What's that?"

He blinked, turned his attention to the woman at his side. She pointed toward the woods to the left of the lake. His gaze followed that path. He squinted. What was she seeing?

She started moving forward again. "In the tree line. I can just make out a structure or cabin."

"But the cabin burned down."

"There," she said, pointing again without slowing her pace in the same direction.

That was when he saw it. A roofline angling downward. How had he never seen this before? Maybe because he'd usually come here in the summer, and this early in the spring there were still a lot of trees with bare limbs, which allowed him to see beyond the tree line.

He was running now, and Reyna was keeping pace with him.

They reached the small cabin. Rustic. Old. How the hell was this here without him noticing? Ben gave the handle a twist and to his surprise the door opened.

"I should have a look first," he suggested.

She gestured to the door. "Hurry. I want to see."

The interior looked dark since the tiny structure sat back in the trees far enough to keep it shaded. The windows were cloudy from years of neglect blocking most of the light that would have penetrated the darkness. He reached for his cell, tapped the flashlight app.

He stepped inside and skimmed the light over the interior. Framed photographs on the walls.

Ben spotted a photo of his dad. He moved closer. There were more. A lot more. He stood in the middle of the cramped space and turned slowly, allowing the light to play over the walls. Dozens of framed photographs—all of them moments captured in time. Moments in the life of the three men who had disappeared. Not the kind taken from a distance the way a stalker would, but the sort snapped by someone with them…someone they knew.

"Look at this." Reyna had turned on her own flashlight app as well. "Their jerseys from high school."

Ben moved to the wall where the three jerseys hung. Numbers 21, Ward; 18, Fuller; and 14, Evans. "This is some sort of shrine."

"Maybe the Widows put all this together," she suggested. "Makes sense with the way it's all laid out."

Why wouldn't his mother tell him about this? He would have loved to share this with her. If she had been embarrassed, she shouldn't have been. He would have understood.

Before exiting the one-room cabin, they scoured the wall a foot at a time. Same with the ceiling and the floor. Both took dozens of pics, documenting the extensive efforts someone had gone to in order to create this memorial. Whoever had built the place had never painted it. Just left the natural wood, well aged and covered in memorabilia dedicated to the three men who had vanished without a trace.

Outside it took a moment for his eyes to adjust to the sunlight. His gut was in knots, and he wanted to call Lucinda and demand to know why she'd never told him. This was his father. Ben had a right to know about this… to see it. Damn it.

"Should we call Sheriff Norwood?"

"We should. Yeah." He doubted this was relevant to how or why they'd disappeared, but he was in no position to make that judgment. He was emotionally compromised, and he was no cop.

Ben studied the structure of the small cabin. It was well-built, not thrown together by novices. The roof was sturdy, and he'd seen no sign of leaks inside. Definitely built to last.

Had his grandfather helped his mother with this?

The quality of the work suggested his grandfather's level of craftsmanship.

He started toward the back of the structure. Reyna had already gone that way.

"Ben!"

The shock or fear in her voice had him rushing around

the rear corner to find her. She stood only a few feet from the back of the cabin in a small clearing that was overgrown with grass and weeds, but it was the three wooden crosses that had him stalling in his tracks.

Moving on autopilot, Ben stamped through the knee-high grass until he reached the crosses. Three in a neat row. No markings or names. Just three rustic crosses.

Ben went down on his knees and pressed his hands to the ground. He felt the surface, touched the wood where it had been driven in the ground.

Could his father and the others be here?

Could they have been here all along?

Reyna knelt beside him, put a hand on his arm. "It's time to call Sheriff Norwood."

3:00 p.m.

SHERIFF NORWOOD AND three of her deputies as well as the lead member of the county's crime scene investigation team had arrived and were going through the cabin and the area around it.

Reyna and Ben had been sequestered a safe distance from the structure. Norwood was not happy that they'd gone inside. But not going inside would have been impossible, even for Reyna. She glanced at Ben. He was tense. Ready to snap. She could understand why. If his father was buried here…had been for all these years…

He didn't want to tell his grandfather anything until they were certain. A good move, in Reyna's opinion. As hard as this was on Ben, it was even harder on the elder Kane.

The point that kept kicking around inside Rey's brain was the idea that Walls had basically sent them here. He had suggested they look at the Fuller property by the lake, and voilà, here was this shrine to the missing husbands. And grave markers. There was just no ignoring the idea that he might have known about this place. Whatever Norwood thought of the deputy, this was not something that could be easily overlooked. Walls had to have known or at the very least had some inkling.

"He knew." Ben turned to her with the words as if she had somehow telegraphed them to him. "This is no coincidence."

"We told Norwood the reason we came here," Reyna agreed. "She won't be able to ignore he had to know this was here."

Ben shook his head. "Why would he keep this from us all this time? What kind of man would do that?"

"One with something to hide," she warned.

Norwood exited the cabin and started in their direction.

"Let's see what she has to say now," he muttered.

"We're going to do some excavating back there. See what we find." She glanced back at the cabin. "There's no need for the two of you to hang around. This is going to take some time. If we find anything, I'll let you know."

"What about Deputy Walls?" Ben demanded, his voice taut with agitation.

"I've called him three times since you told me how you found this, but he's not answering. I've issued a BOLO for him, his private vehicle and his county SUV. We'll find him, and then we'll get some answers. Meanwhile, it would be best if you don't discuss this with anyone for now. We need to talk to your grandfather and to your mother," she said to Ben. "We need to find out what they knew before they hear about your finding it and our being here."

“They would have told me,” Ben argued. “There is no way either of them knew about this.”

Norwood nodded. “Maybe. But those photographs came from people close to those men. Either they were stolen from their homes or…” She exhaled a big breath. “You get where I’m going.”

“I got it,” Ben agreed.

“Call us,” Reyna urged, “as soon as you find anything. It’s been thirty years. They don’t need to wait a minute longer than necessary.”

Chapter Nine

Kane Residence
Lula Lake Lane
5:30 p.m.

Ben felt like he was in a sort of shock. He stared at the cup of coffee his grandfather had made for him. Somehow he'd lost interest, couldn't think about anything else. Finding that shrine to the Three…had emotions erupting inside him that he didn't fully understand. The anger and frustration he got. Thirty years was a long time to wait for the truth. But it was the other, the uncertainty, that he couldn't comprehend. The truth was what he'd waited his whole life to find, right?

Then why the hell did he suddenly feel like everything was about to change—and not for the better?

He'd tried calling his mother, and she wasn't answering. They'd dropped by her house and gotten no response there either. Her car was in the garage, but that didn't mean she was home. She could have gone to the city with a friend, one of the other widows. Frankly, they were the only friends he'd ever seen her do things with. Not so much in the past few years. If he looked long and hard at the situation, he would have to say that beyond Ms. Fuller and Ms. Evans, his mother had no actual friends. She went to church and did her shopping around town and was always friendly to everyone but never went to dinner or other outings with anyone or invited anyone to the house.

Growing up, he hadn't really noticed because the Widows had always been together. He'd had his grandfather and he'd had his friends from school. But looking back, he recognized that his mother had had a lonely existence beyond her association with the Widows. She never dated anyone. Never went on trips, cruises—nothing.

He tried calling her again. The call went directly to voice mail.

"She still not answering?" his grandfather asked. He pushed his own untouched cup of coffee aside.

Ben ended the call and tossed his cell onto the table. "Maybe she's with Sheriff Norwood. But the sheriff said she'd let me know when she spoke to her."

"She came here straightaway," his grandfather reminded him. "I'm sure she went in search of Lucinda immediately after speaking to me or maybe before."

"I suppose it's possible Norwood has spoken with her and Mom doesn't want to talk about it." His mother was like that—she didn't enjoy revisiting what had happened. Frankly, Ben was still stunned that she had opened up to Reyna as much as she had. For a little while she'd talked freely, and then she'd closed up once more. He just didn't get any of this.

He looked at his grandfather then. "How did we not know about the cabin?" Ben shook his head. "Ms. Fuller had to know. Gordon Walls sure seemed to know. He's fallen off the radar now too. Sheriff Norwood couldn't reach him."

"I wish I knew, son." Ward gave an affirming nod. "I

certainly had no idea. But we need to find out how that cabin came about. I'd say we need answers more than ever before."

Reyna walked into the room holding one of the old photo albums. She'd given Ben and his grandfather some privacy to discuss the find and how things had gone with Norwood. She hadn't exactly said that was what she was doing, but she'd wanted to look at photo albums again while they'd talked in the kitchen. Ben appreciated the space she'd given them. Not that he'd believed for one minute that his grandfather knew about that place by the lake. No way.

"I'm assuming," she said as she settled into one of the available chairs and placed the album on the table, "that all the teammates and the coach were questioned. Probably more than once."

"They were," Ward said. "Even though JR, Duke and Judson hadn't really stayed in contact with the others, every person they had known in high school, college and in their work lives was questioned. The football team in particular," he went on, "since those young men had all grown up here together. Most had moved to the city or surrounding area, but..." He made an aha face. "The reunion. Just a few months before the disappearance, JR attended his ten-year high school reunion. They all three did. I think the sheriff and the deputies investigating the disappearance hoped someone from the reunion would remember something one of them said."

"Did anything happen at the reunion that prompted the police to think this?" Reyna closed the photo album, her full attention on Ward now.

He frowned, struggling to remember probably. Ben had been a kid. He had forgotten all about the reunion until his grandfather had mentioned it. But now he vaguely recalled that there had been some disagreement between his dad and his mother about him not wanting to wear his team jersey.

"My parents argued about Dad's team jersey," Ben said, his mind still focused on thirty years ago. His mother had been furious, but Ben couldn't remember why. He could see her face…could see her clutching the jersey. The one—or one just like it—that hung in the cabin they had found. The memory had to mean something. His gut clenched. None of this could be coincidence. "I don't know if the argument was before or after the reunion."

"There was some argument at the reunion," Ward explained. His forehead furrowed as if he was working hard to recall some fact. "I remember now. One of the other guys who had played with JR and the others was bragging about how Coach Landon had insisted that his boy had that special something. The kid was going places. Anyway, Landon and Duke exchanged some heated words. If I'm remembering right, I think Coach Landon even left early that night."

Didn't make a lot of sense to Ben. "Duke didn't have any kids. I can't see him being jealous of what some guy said about his kid's performance on the team. There had to be something more than that, Pops."

Ward turned his hands up. "I'm just telling you how the story went as it made its way around town—at least, what I remember of it. Your daddy and your mama refused to talk about it, so I can't say anything with any measurable accuracy. The whole thing blew over." His gaze grew distant. "And then they were gone."

"We should talk to the coach," Reyna suggested.

"I'm not so sure that would be worth our time and

trouble," Ben explained. "Landon is wheelchair bound and a bit of a shut-in. Who knows how his memory is?"

"It's not like we're accomplishing anything sitting around here waiting," Reyna contended.

"She's right," his grandfather said. "The two of you should see what Landon can recall. I'll be here if you need backup." He chuckled. "Plus, I'll go around and check on your mama. Make sure she's okay—assuming I can find her."

Ben looked to Reyna. "Let's do it."

Landon Residence
Harding Drive
6:15 p.m.

THE LONGTIME FOOTBALL coach of Whispering Winds had retired just over twenty-nine years ago, after his home had burned to the ground. An electrical issue had started the fire, according to the articles Reyna had found on the internet. The man had been forced to jump from a second-story window to escape the fire. The injuries he'd sustained had been the reason he was wheelchair bound.

Reyna had called Landon and laid it on a little thick about needing to interview him for her next book. She'd played to his ego—considering everything she'd read from his heyday in coaching, the man appeared to have had a rather large one. No surprise there. It took a lot of ego for a man to take a bunch of kids, shape them into a team and then ensure they won more often than not.

Whatever his formula, it had been a successful one.

According to one article written a couple of years ago about the high school football team, they hadn't experienced a true winning streak since Landon had been forced to retire. His record of victories remained unbroken.

Reyna wasn't really interested in his coaching prowess. She wanted to understand the Three better from the perspective of a man who had known them well and who wasn't connected by blood or marriage. More importantly, she wanted to know why he and Duke Fuller had exchanged heated words at the ten-year reunion.

Ben parked in front of a small cottage along a short street lined with similar little cottages. Other than color, they all looked basically alike. Small. Neat and colorful enough to have been on a beach in Florida.

"I'm assuming we shouldn't mention the cabin," Ben said as they walked toward the man's door.

"Agreed." Reyna paused before reaching the entrance. She'd spotted the doorbell camera, which meant once near the door, the man inside could most likely see and hear them. "I'll take the lead, if that's okay with you. You've seen the man around. You certainly know him better than I do. I'd like you to watch him closely. When we're done, tell me if you think he was being completely honest with his answers or if anything I ask affects his emotions."

Ben nodded. "I can do that."

She walked the remaining steps to the door and knocked. The knob turned and the door opened. Coach Wade Landon rolled backward in his wheelchair.

"Saw the two of you on my doorbell camera. Come on in."

"Thank you for making the time to see us," Reyna said. She gestured to Ben as he closed the door. "I'm sure you know Ben Kane. He has kindly agreed to show me around town and introduce me to the folks."

"I sure do. His daddy was the best running back we ever had."

Ben smiled, though it wasn't one of his full-blown charmers. Reyna had come to appreciate his genuine smiles probably more than she should have.

He was a nice man. Handsome. Kind. How was it she'd never been lucky enough to meet a guy like him in her real life? Reyna banished the idea. This was real life. Just not hers. Well, it sort of was. This was her work.

"The living room is straight through here," Landon said as he turned his wheelchair around in the relatively wide entrance hall and headed toward the back of the cottage.

Reyna exchanged a look with Ben before following. She had a feeling this investigation was beginning to get to him in a way he hadn't expected. She wished it wasn't necessary to put him through these steps. But her first obligation was to Eudora.

The idea sat like a stone in her stomach.

Was it really?

Or was her first obligation to finding the truth for all concerned?

That conclusion seemed to suggest she had some special superpower that she didn't. All she could hope for was to dig around enough and turn over all the necessary rocks and maybe find something no one else had.

Like that cabin.

The realization still stunned her. Someone had built what could only be called a shrine to the Three. On Fuller property, no less.

Who? Why? When? How had the Fullers not known?

Then again, maybe they did.

Either way, Reyna wanted to find those answers. She'd wanted to track down Ms. Fuller and try again for an interview, but the discovery of the cabin had waylaid that possibility. The sheriff wanted to talk to her and to Ms. Evans first—the same as they had Ward and Lucinda. Now any additional interviews of the Widows were postponed until after the official notification and questioning was done.

"Sit anywhere you like," Landon said as he parked next to a table that was clearly where he spent a good deal of his time. A cell phone lay on the table. Next to that was a pair of glasses and, most important of all, the television remote.

"Coach," Reyna said as she settled on the sofa, "tell us about the Three around the time of the ten-year high school reunion."

He looked surprised at her question. "We mostly lost touch after high school," he said, choosing his words carefully. "I knew them better back in those days." He propped a smile into place, but it wasn't the same broad, open one he'd been wearing when he'd answered the door.

"They were good students," Reyna suggested. "Good team players. You had high hopes for Duke Fuller."

He nodded, lips in a tight line. "I did. Duke could have gone pro. Instead, he blew off his college opportunity and, well…you know."

"There was trouble at the reunion," Reyna ventured. "An argument broke out."

If possible, the man's face paled more so than it already was. He clearly didn't leave the house much.

"I had left by then." He shrugged. "Reunions are for the students. Some of us showed up for the first hour or so. It's expected."

Ben spoke up. "I was told that Duke Fuller was upset by something one of his old classmates said about his son and you."

A slow, stiff nod from Landon. "Oh, yes. I remember something about that." He shrugged. "Bradley Carson. His son, Jesse, had a very promising ability. Just a natural. I know a good player when I see one. I was lucky to be able to get the boy started when he was just a tyke in peewee football. I sort of recruited him. You may not be aware, but I helped out with the local peewee team. It was a pleasure to volunteer my time with those kids. Anyway, Duke and Carson had words that night. I don't know if what was said somehow made Duke jealous or what. The behavior was completely unexpected and actually very much out of character for him. That's all I know."

"Why would Duke," Reyna ventured, "have an issue with your praise of someone else's child? It just seems strange since he had no children. Why do you suppose he overreacted?"

Landon shrugged again. "Who knows? I think he'd been drinking, and maybe it bothered him that I had said the same things about him in his playing days, but he threw the opportunity away. The truth is I can't really say. I wasn't there at that point."

"What made you think he'd been drinking?" Ben asked.

More shrugging from Landon. "His words were slurred early on—before I left. He was kind of rude to me and my wife, if I'm being totally honest. Duke could be mean like that. As for why he would be jealous of Carson's kid, maybe it was about you." His gaze settled on Ben. "Your daddy didn't want you to play. Maybe Duke thought you should have and that you'd have been better than Jesse. I guess we'll never know."

"That's so strange," Reyna said. "Everyone I've interviewed said it was you who had that heated exchange with Duke."

The coach shook his head. "I mean, we talked, but I wouldn't call it heated. Like I said, my wife and I left."

"Only a few days after the reunion, your wife had her accident," Reyna said, moving on.

His face turned sad. "She did. Got up in the middle of the night to go downstairs for a glass of water and fell. It was the worst night of my life."

"Then the Three disappeared, and no one's life was the same," Ben said.

Landon nodded but kept his attention on his hands, which were clasped in his lap.

When neither man spoke for a bit, Reyna said, "The fire was nearly a year later."

Landon's gaze lifted to hers. "After my wife died, at least I still had my work, but then I lost that too."

"The report," she went on, "showed that you woke up to the house in flames and your only option to save yourself was to jump out a second-story window."

"I couldn't get down the stairs." He shuddered. "The smoke was so thick I could barely breathe. It was *go out the window or die*."

"The fire marshal's report showed there were no accelerants of any sort in the house. The fire started and just kept going. No alarms notified the fire department, and your house was a fair distance from any others on the street."

"With me asleep—my neighbors too—no one noticed until it was too late."

"Your body was bruised, and there were a good many wounds," she noted, recalling all that she'd read when digging around in his past.

"My memories of that night are scattered, fuzzy, but the docs said I probably bounced off the side of the house and the porch roof. I was meaning to jump to the porch roof and then to the ground, but that didn't work out." He gestured to his chair. "All this damage occurred in that sudden stop when I hit the ground."

"It was a miracle you survived," she agreed.

He nodded.

"Had you been drinking that night?" she asked. "Maybe taken sleeping pills?" One article she'd read suggested he may have taken sleep medication, but the reporter had only been speculating.

"I don't drink," he said quickly. "Never have. I had sleeping pills. They weren't mine—they were my wife's. I may have taken one. I really don't remember. My wife always took them. I had trouble sleeping after she was gone."

"Is there anything at all," Reyna said, "you recall about the Three that might help us in our search for answers about their disappearance?"

He moved his head slowly from side to side. "I wish there was. They were good kids who grew up to be good men. It's a darn shame the police or the FBI have never figured out what happened to them."

Reyna couldn't agree more. It was a shame. The worst part was that someone somewhere—more than likely right here in Whispering Winds—knew exactly what had happened.

Maybe even this man who had known them so well. Who could say? The one thing Reyna suspected was without doubt correct was that he was not being completely honest.

As she and Ben walked back to his truck, she asked, "What were your impressions in there?"

Ben opened her door and then looked her straight in the eyes. "He was lying."

Exactly what Reyna had thought.

The Jewel Bed & Breakfast
Main Street
7:00 p.m.

THE CLEANUP CREW had done a spectacular job on the downstairs areas. Thankfully the smoke damage was minimal there. The bigger problem was in the room that had been Reyna's. There was fire, smoke and water destruction. The second-floor rooms would need a thorough and specific cleaning to remedy the smoke odor. But for the most part, the actual mess was confined to the one room.

"I'm so glad this isn't as bad as we feared," Reyna said to the woman who had become a fast friend.

"You and me both." Birdie nodded. "I'm extra grateful that it didn't happen at night while we were all sleeping."

The way it had for Coach Landon. He was lucky to be alive. Reyna thought of the wheelchair and wondered if there were times when he didn't feel so lucky.

Ben had gotten a call and was pacing the lobby. Birdie had ushered Reyna to the small parlor in her private quarters. The rooms were lovely and oh so vintage, with lots of color and sparkle, just like the woman.

"It's a little late for tea," she said. "Would you like a drink of something stronger?"

Reyna hesitated only a second. Then she nodded. "You know, I think I would love something stronger."

While Birdie prepared their drinks, Reyna wandered around her parlor and admired all the lovely framed photographs. So many were of her and Eudora. Clearly, they had been dear friends for a very long time.

On the mantel was a photo taken at the beach what appeared to be maybe fifty years ago. The intimate moment snagged and held Rey's attention. The two were holding hands. But that wasn't the thing… The thing was the way they looked at each other over their cocktail glasses.

Reyna's breath caught ever so slightly, and her heart started to pound.

"Here we go."

She set the photograph back in its place on the mantel and accepted the shot glass of something that looked and smelled quite strong.

"Bottoms up," Birdie said with a wink.

They turned up their glasses at the same time. The sweet burn rushed down Reyna's throat, and she barely stifled a cough.

"Oh, that had some heat to it." She laughed. "But it was certainly good."

Birdie winked. "It gets better."

Reyna gestured to the photograph. "You and Eudora love each other."

Birdie's gaze rested on the photograph. "We always have. Some days she doesn't remember, but I will cherish our every memory for the rest of my life."

"In love," Reyna clarified. "The two of you are a couple."

Birdie smiled. "In some places." She gestured to the photo. "The way we were in that shot in Cancún. But not here. Never here."

Reyna scoffed. "Please, there is no reason for you two to hide the way you feel. The world has changed."

She nodded. "It has, but sometimes in small towns it's easier to go with the way things have always been. Fifty-five years ago she was a schoolteacher and I was a wanderer trying to find my place. The way we found each other and lived our lives never mattered as long as we were together. We were happy and loved each other until I could no longer properly take care of Eudora at home.

Then she insisted I take her to the center, and I visit her every chance I get. We speak by phone every night that she's lucid enough to do so." The older woman took a deep breath. "She accuses me of not coming to see her anymore, but it's only because she doesn't remember I was there." She smiled sadly as she touched the faces in the treasured photo. "She will live in my heart just like this forever."

"I hope the two of you will allow me to find a way to incorporate your beautiful secret into her story."

"That is entirely up to Dory."

"I wish your friends in the community could have known and celebrated with you." Reyna sensed no resentment in Birdie.

"The only person who ever knew was Father Cullen." She laughed. "He knows everyone's secrets. Dory and I always called him the secret keeper." She shrugged. "I had moments when I was certain Ward Kane knew, but if he did he never said a word."

Reyna hugged her as firmly as she dared. The woman was eighty, after all. "Thank you for sharing your secret with me."

Later, Birdie walked Reyna and Ben to the porch and waved as they drove away.

"She's such a lovely woman," Reyna said, enthralled with the love story of Birdie and Eudora. "I want to be so calm and accepting. To live the life I have and not wait for some other thing to happen or come along."

Ben laughed. "I think you're doing just fine on the path you're traveling."

She laughed too. "I'll take that as a huge compliment, Mr. Kane."

"That was Sheriff Norwood who called. They found nothing buried in the back of the cabin. They're still trying to collect and prepare all the fingerprints for running through the system. A lot of local folks provided their prints thirty years ago, so she'll compare all those. She still hasn't been able to track down Mom. I tried calling her and it just goes to voice mail."

"That's so frustrating." Reyna had really hoped there would be something at the cabin. She wasn't really surprised his mother was avoiding the news. She felt sure Ben wasn't surprised either. As for the lack of discovery at the cabin, Reyna wasn't calling it done yet. There had to be answers they could find. She refused to accept any other conclusion. And that cabin was connected somehow. "They could still find something useful. We should keep the faith until there are no other options. Forensics can do magic these days."

Ben parked in the driveway at his home. The lights downstairs were on, except for the one on the east end that was in Mr. Kane's bedroom.

They sat in the dark silence for a bit. Reyna was waiting for Ben to make a move toward getting out of the truck. Maybe he was waiting for the same. Whatever the case, the two of them just sitting there quietly felt right for now.

Finally, she decided to mention, "Birdie said Father Cullen knew everyone's secrets. She and Eudora called him the secret keeper."

Ben chuckled softly. "Makes sense."

She turned to him. "This has been a really tough day for you. I'm sorry. I feel a little like it's my fault."

He shifted in his seat to face her. "No. It's not your fault. It just is. Is the fact that you're here poking around making things happen? It seems so. Are those things uncomfortable? A little. But they need to happen. We need the truth."

She put her hand on his arm, resisted a shiver at the tingle that fired where their skin touched. "We're going to find the answers. I won't stop until I do or you run me off."

He took her hand in his and traced her fingers with his own. "I don't think I could bring myself to run you off under any circumstances."

She laughed, the sound nervous. "Maybe you just need more time in the same house with me. I'm used to doing things my own way. I can be—"

Before she could finish, his mouth had closed over hers, and then he pulled back as if asking permission. She nodded, and he resumed. The kiss was soft and deep and over far too quickly.

"I probably should have warned you that I'd been dying to do that since the first time I laid eyes on you."

Her nerves were jangling and her body was shaking, but she wasn't ready to run… She was ready for more.

"Maybe you can do it again, just to be sure you scratched that itch."

He kissed her again, and this time it went on and on.

Chapter Ten

Kane Residence
Lula Lake Lane
Thursday, April 25, 6:45 a.m.

Ben opened his eyes and stared at the woman in bed next to him.

He had not seen that one coming. He'd thought about it, for sure, but he hadn't figured out whether she was drawn to him the way he was to her.

He wanted to touch her so badly…run his hands through that mass of red hair. It was spread across the white pillowcase like flames. Those freckles he'd noticed the first time he'd seen her seemed to become more vivid when she was alive with desire the way she had been last night. He'd tried kissing each one but his lips had just kept finding their way to her mouth, and then they'd gotten lost in the fever again.

Apparently, a guy never got too mature to be blown away by a woman's body…by her touch…her scent…and the way she looked at him. Like he was all she had ever wanted.

Whoa. He had to slow it down here. This was no romance movie—this was real life, and they were in the middle of a major mess that had roots deep in his life.

He doubted either of them would feel the same when the tension of finding answers was past.

His gaze flowed over the shape of her beneath that sheet, and his mouth went dry. Right now he couldn't see ever feeling anything less than a frantic need to touch her.

Her eyes fluttered open, and that brilliant green took his breath.

God, she was beautiful.

"Morning," he murmured.

"Morning." She smiled. "I think I may have lost my objectivity last night."

He grinned. "Just a little bit, maybe."

He'd lost his mind, and he'd loved every single minute of it.

"Will you be comfortable with me staying here after this?" she asked, her eyes searching his face for reaction.

He traced her cheek with his fingers, swept a lock of hair back. "I won't be comfortable with you anywhere else."

"Good." She smiled again. "I don't know about you, but I'm absolutely starving."

"As it happens," he said, bracing his elbow on his pillow and his head in his hand, "I am a very good cook. My pops taught me how to fend for myself."

"That means—" she sat up "—that I get the shower first."

She jumped out of bed and rushed toward the bathroom, laughing and pulling the sheet around her as she went, leaving him buck naked on the bed. He liked her laugh too. She might have gotten first dibs on his shower, but there was another one downstairs. Even a few steps behind, he would still finish first and have bacon cooking in a pan when she appeared in the kitchen.

HALF AN HOUR later Ben had the bacon frying and the biscuits in the oven. Making biscuits from scratch was one culinary feat he had not mastered. In an effort to avoid early morning disasters, his grandfather had shared his biscuit-making secret—the frozen ones could be just as good with the right amount of butter slathered on.

Ben frowned. Speaking of which, where was the guy? He was usually up before Ben. He tossed the oven mitt aside and would have headed to his grandfather's bedroom, but he spotted a sticky note on the back-door glass, just barely visible beyond the curtain. When Ben had been in high school, his grandfather had stuck notes on the door glass to ensure he'd seen them before leaving for the day. If Ben overslept, he might not go to the coffee maker or the fridge, but he had to walk out the door.

Checking on a few things. See you tonight.

Ben frowned. Usually his grandfather talked to him about his plans for the day. Maybe the news about the cabin had upset him more than Ben had realized. He should have gone to his room and checked on him last night.

But he'd been too busy with…

"Damn." He tossed the note onto the counter and went back to the stove to turn the bacon.

"Smells great." Reyna walked into the kitchen in borrowed jeans that fit her as if she'd had them made just for her and one of Birdie's flashy, low-cut shirts hugging her breasts—body.

"Coffee's ready." He forced his attention back on the frying pan. "The rest will be in about two minutes."

"Sheriff Norwood called me." She paused at the coffee maker and grabbed the mug Ben had set out for her.

"She needs my fingerprints to rule me out of the dozens her team has lifted."

"We can go by the substation first thing," he said. Norwood would likely want Reyna's prints sooner rather than later.

"Great." She savored her coffee for a moment. "I thought we might stop by the cemetery, if you're comfortable with that."

The idea gave him pause, but he pushed through it. "We can do that."

His father and his friends had been buried in the Whispering Winds cemetery, the one that was as old as the town. Of course, there had been no bodies in their coffins, only a few pieces of memorabilia. The families hadn't even declared them dead until a few years ago. No one had wanted to take that step.

It wasn't until Duke Fuller's grandfather had passed away that the family attorney had said they'd needed to do this right—the grandfather's property could not pass down to Ms. Fuller until Duke had been declared dead. The same with Judson Evans, except his mother had still been alive and she hadn't really wanted to do it. But when Lucinda had joined the *let's get it over with* side, Ms. Evans had gone along.

Putting aside the painful thoughts, he and Reyna ate, talked, laughed. It was comfortable. Surprisingly so. Ben had expected the morning after to be awkward, but Reyna didn't let that happen. Just something else he liked about her.

He wondered if she would think about him after she was gone. She had a life, a job. She would be getting back to all that. This was just a layover for research.

But it sure felt like more to him. Then again, he was pretty rusty at this romance thing.

Whispering Winds Cemetery
9:00 a.m.

REYNA SAT ON the bench that had been installed by the high school alumni in memory of the three classmates who had vanished.

The three headstones were the same. Black marble with silver etching revealing the names, dates of birth and death—disappearance, actually—as well as epitaphs for the memory of those entombed there, because memory was all they'd had to bury. The idea that none of the three families had been in a hurry to take this legal step seemed to indicate they wanted nothing that might feel like they were gaining from the deaths. No death benefits of any sort, including insurance. They wanted to go on pretending that the three men might come back one day.

Could Reyna say with absolute certainty that the Three were dead? Of course she couldn't. But it had been thirty years without a trace. The odds were against them being alive.

That said, it did happen. Most of those cases involved people who didn't want to be found. Nothing Reyna had uncovered suggested that was the case with the Three.

Ben sat down beside her. "I keep seeing those handmade crosses, and I can't help wondering who put them there. More importantly, why?" He gestured to the markers in front of them. "This was done nearly a decade ago. I mean, I guess it's possible what was done at that cabin goes back further than ten years. Forensics is working on putting some dates together, according to Norwood."

In the past three days, Reyna had learned a great deal about the people left behind, but she hadn't learned as much about the Three—the men who had actually disappeared.

"Tell me about your father." She turned to Ben and studied his handsome profile. He looked so very much like the photos of his father. If the man was anything like this one, he had been a great guy.

"He was always smiling. He..." Ben smiled, and Reyna's heart stumbled. "He had this laugh, kind of a low rumble that was contagious. Everyone—and I mean everyone—liked him. I honestly have never met anyone who didn't like him. If they knew him, they liked him."

"Do you ever remember him and your mother fighting?"

Ben shook his head. "Never. I mean, I'm sure they did, but they kept it private. My mom has never bad-mouthed him. I'd think by now if he'd ever given her any trouble I would have heard about it." He frowned. "But there was something around the time of the reunion that caused a disagreement. That meeting with the coach jarred the hint of a memory, but I haven't been able to grasp it yet."

"I think it's a reasonable assumption that your parents were happy. What about his relationship with his friends Duke and Judson? Any talk of trouble between them?" There was nothing in the many, many interviews and statements floating out there in cyberspace. But put three guys together playing sports and dating, it made sense that they wouldn't always see eye to eye.

"Pops told me once that the three of them used to work out any issues in the woods."

"In the woods?"

He nodded. "They would take off in different directions and run as long and hard as they could. When they couldn't run any further, they had to stop and find their way back to each other. It gave them time to think about what was real, distance to give them perspective, and the hard run drained the adrenaline. By the time they found each other, whatever the trouble had been, it didn't matter anymore."

What an ingenious idea. "Your grandfather is brilliant."

"He is. He thinks things through. Doesn't take sides."

"Have you spoken to him this morning?"

Ben shook his head. "He'd already left when I got downstairs. I'm a little worried. He doesn't usually avoid me."

Reyna was really sorry to hear this. "I'm certain it's not really about avoiding you. He may just need to work this for himself." She considered what she'd learned from the coach and the trouble that had cropped up at the ten-year reunion. "Has he ever mentioned anything about Coach Landon? Likes, dislikes? Doubts?"

"Pops has never talked about him in particular. In my experience, if he has nothing to say about someone, then he doesn't like them very much."

Made sense to Reyna. "I wish we had more information about what happened at the class reunion." That was the biggest hole in the puzzle she was putting together.

"I was thinking about what Coach suggested was the reason for the argument that night," Ben said. "You know, the Jesse Carson thing. Jesse was, like, three years older than me, but I vaguely remember him because he was the only boy born to anyone on the team besides me. All the others who grew up, got married and had children had girls." He put up his hands. "Don't ask why that particular fact occurred to me, but it did."

"We need to find out what that disagreement was about," Reyna pointed out. "It suddenly seems significant."

"Well, we could try talking to Ms. Fuller again," Ben offered. "We kind of skipped over that second attempt with all that's happened."

"I think that's a great idea." She stood. Surely the sheriff had spoken to Fuller by now. "Let's go for a cold call and see what kind of reaction we get."

Fuller Residence
Hawk's Way
10:30 a.m.

BEN DECIDED DEIDRE FULLER was hiding from them. Her garage was closed and without windows, leaving no way to know if her car was there. But she wasn't answering the door or her cell phone.

"Well," Reyna announced, "we tried."

Ben surveyed the house and yard. "We'll try again later."

He was not giving up until he talked to her about the things they had learned.

They had just reached his truck when another vehicle arrived. Truck. White. Tinted windows. Newer than Ben's. When the driver's-side door opened and a man emerged, Ben recognized him. Jesse Carson. Talk about a bizarre coincidence. Jesse and his family had moved to Nashville eons ago. Maybe six months or so after the Three had disappeared. It wasn't until this moment—after learning about the disagreement at the reunion—that their move seemed in any way relevant.

But that could very well be wishful thinking.

"Kane," the other man said as he strode toward Ben. "I haven't seen you since— God, I don't even know when." He thrust out his hand, glanced at Reyna as he did so.

Ben gave his hand a shake. "It's been a while, for sure."

He motioned toward the house. "I hope Ms. Fuller is in a good mood. I need to talk to her about her financial portfolio, and unfortunately none of it's good."

"You still working for that big-time wealth-building company?" Now that portfolios were mentioned, Ben vaguely remembered hearing about Carson winning some sort of award in the world of finance.

"I do, but it's a struggle in this economy."

"We knocked on her door, but there's no answer," Ben explained. "She's either out or avoiding us."

Jesse glanced at Reyna for the second time.

Ben gave himself a mental kick. "Sorry. This is Reyna Hart." He gestured to Jesse. "Jesse Carson." He gave her a look that said *you know the one*. "His father was on the team with the Three."

"Nice to meet you." Reyna shook his hand. "You played football around here too?"

"When I was just a little kid. We moved to Nashville when I was ten." He frowned then. "Now, why would someone as nice as Ms. Fuller be avoiding the two of you?"

"My bad." Ben explained, "Reyna and I are looking into the disappearance of the Three. We're actually making a little headway."

"No kidding," Jesse said. "Wow. It's crazy that thirty years later we still don't know what happened. My dad still talks about them."

"For sure," Ben agreed.

"Does your father ever talk about what happened?" Reyna asked.

Jesse turned to her. "I mean, he's talked about it from time to time, but not so much, really. Nothing in particular that I remember. Wait." He held up a hand. "There was this one thing I remember vividly. I guess I was, like, ten—it was just before we moved, in fact. Coach Landon had handpicked me from the peewee team to start on the middle school team a year early. I was super excited. It was a big deal to get picked for the team early by one of the most popular coaches in the state."

Ben frowned. "I don't remember you playing on the middle school team."

"I didn't. My dad pitched a heck of a fit. My mother would never tell me the details. I was pretty upset. But my parents just kept saying they didn't want me to play for Landon. So I didn't. In fact, we moved right around that same time—right after your dad and the others disappeared." He frowned. "Or maybe right before. Man, thirty years. I feel old now."

"I'm sure they had a good reason for not wanting you to play," Reyna offered, hoping to prompt more from him.

"Guess so." Jesse looked from her to Ben. "Well, it was good to see you, but I have to run. If you see Ms. Fuller, tell her I stopped by." He shook his head. "She's the only client I have in this neck of the woods, but Dad insisted I take her on as a client. I guess he thought she might need a trustworthy adviser. He said he owed her a big favor."

"Will do," Ben said. "It was good to see you too."

When Jesse had driven away and Ben and Reyna had climbed into his truck, she said, "Duke, your father and Judson played football their entire school careers, for Coach Landon. Why the explosion when he learned a teammate's son—the only son born to the group—was going to follow in their footsteps?"

"No idea." Ben shrugged. "It makes no sense at all."

"Exactly," Reyna confirmed. "We should ask Landon. Maybe if we tell him we spoke to Jesse Carson he'll be more forthcoming."

"Can't hurt to try."

As Ben headed in the direction of the coach's home, Reyna pulled her cell phone from her pocket to answer an incoming call. She listened for half a minute and then promised the caller she would be right there.

When she'd disconnected, she turned to Ben. "I have to get to Eudora. Can you take me back to get my SUV?"

"No need." He sent her a sidelong look. "I'll take you."

The only thing that worried him more than the idea that at some point Reyna would leave was the notion of letting her out of his sight until he had no other choice.

The Light Memory Care Center
Lantern Pointe
Chattanooga
Noon

WHEN THEY REACHED Eudora's room, Rey's heart surged into her throat. She looked so frail…so pale.

As they'd headed out of Whispering Winds, Reyna had somehow had the presence of mind to ask Ben to go by the Jewel and pick up Birdie. The three of them had ridden in silence the entire half hour it had taken to reach the facility.

Reyna waited for Birdie to approach Eudora first. The worry on her face hurt to watch. She took Eudora's hand in her own, and the frail woman's eyes fluttered open.

"My sweet Dory, tell me you're staying with me, please."

Eudora's nearly translucent fingers curled around Birdie's. "I'll always be with you, Bird. I'm just tired now, and I need to rest."

The words gored Reyna. Eudora had never talked so negatively about hanging in there.

"I brought friends to see you," Birdie said. She motioned for Reyna and Ben to join her. "Reyna is with me. She's working on the story, just like you wanted."

"Reyna." The elderly woman's eyes lit just a little. "I'm so glad you came. I need to tell you something, dear. It's very important."

"I'm listening, Eudora," Reyna assured her.

"I should have told you they would try to stop you. Birdie told me the things they've done."

"Who are *they*, Eudora?" Reyna asked. "I can't protect myself if I don't know who they are."

Eudora's expression fell. She looked beyond Reyna, and her frown deepened. "JR?"

Reyna's heart stumbled. She thought Ben was his father. "Eudora, it's—"

Eudora waved her off with one feeble hand. "Come closer, JR," she ordered, her voice stronger than before.

Ben moved closer. "Ms. Eudora, you're sounding stronger."

"JR, you need to tell that wife of yours that I'm onto her. I know what she did, and I fear she's in danger because of it."

He exchanged a look with Reyna. "Yes, ma'am, I'll tell her."

Eudora turned back to Reyna. She blinked slowly. "Are you listening, dear?"

"I am, but you never told me who I should be afraid of."

"Good gracious, have you not been hearing me? The Widows. You have to be careful because they will try to stop you."

Chapter Eleven

The Jewel Bed & Breakfast
Whispering Winds
3:30 p.m.

"I should walk you in," Ben suggested.

Birdie waved him off. "I'll be fine." She swiped at her eyes. "Thank you so much," she said to Reyna, "to both of you, for taking me with you."

Reyna reached for her hand, gave it a squeeze. "I wouldn't have left you out for the world."

"We'll just hang around and make sure you get inside okay," Ben said, determined to see that the lady made it into her bed-and-breakfast safely.

Birdie waved as she traveled the cobblestone path. She climbed the steps and crossed the porch. She unlocked the door—Sheriff Norwood had convinced her it was best—and stepped inside.

When the door had closed behind her, Reyna turned to Ben. "We need to find your grandfather and see if he can make sense of what Eudora said about your mother and the Widows and anything at all he remembers about the Carson family's abrupt move."

Ben's face told the story of the emotions whirling inside

him. They had tried repeatedly to reach his grandfather as well as his mother, and neither was answering their calls.

"Part of me wants to go to my mother's house and demand answers. The other part is still worried about Pops's early morning disappearing act. Something is going on with that man. He never does this kind of thing."

"Let's see if he's back home now." Reyna reached for the truck door, but Ben got it first. He opened the door for her.

"Thanks." She smiled when he lingered before closing the door. "Is there something you need to say?"

He stared at the sidewalk a moment. "I don't understand what's going on around here right now, but if it all means the truth is finally coming to the surface—I'm glad." His gaze connected with hers then. "And I'm glad you're part of it."

She laughed softly. "Don't go getting all sappy on me, Mr. Kane. We're not finished yet."

He smiled, then hustled around the hood to climb behind the steering wheel.

Reyna kept her biggest concern to herself. Whatever truth or part of the story that was coming next might not be anything Ben wanted to know. If that turned out to be the case, he likely would wish he'd never laid eyes on her.

The latter was the part that worried Reyna the most.

Kane Residence
Lula Lake Lane
4:00 p.m.

THE HOUSE LOOKED exactly as they'd left it. Ward Kane's truck was still gone. No new note from him on the counter or the door. No indication he'd been back.

Reyna watched Ben struggle with what to do next. The worry on his face had her wishing there was more she could do beyond offering moral support.

"Why don't you call your mom again, leave a message asking if she's seen or spoken to Ward. Maybe she'll call you back if she realizes you're worried about your grandfather. I'll call Birdie and ask her to check around with mutual friends. This is a small town. Someone must have seen or heard from one or both of them today."

Unless they don't want to be heard from.

Reyna kept that part to herself. Something else Ben didn't need to hear.

She stepped into the front hall to make her call and to give Ben some privacy for calling his mother.

Birdie's cell went to voice mail, so Reyna called the bed-and-breakfast number. When it went to voice mail as well, she left a message.

"Hey, Birdie, Ward Kane is still not home, and he hasn't called. Ben is worried about him. We haven't been able to reach Lucinda either. Can you check with friends and see if anyone has spoken to or seen them today? Thanks."

Reyna wandered to the parlor and walked around the room, admiring the many family photos. The family looked so happy in those photos. There were so many of JR growing up and plenty more of him and his young family. Ward's wife had been a beautiful woman. There were lots of photos of her and Ward when they'd been younger.

Where were the photos of JR and his football team? The jersey he'd worn had been hanging in that cabin, so it had been kept all those years. And what about photos of him with his two best friends?

Reyna made her way back to the front hall and surveyed the photos there. No team photos. No photos of JR and his friends.

She climbed the stairs, scanning the tread-to-ceiling framed photos hanging there as well. Again, there were none of what she was looking for. Upstairs, she went to the guest room where she was supposed to sleep. She smiled. She kind of liked Ben's bed better. No photos of the team or friends there either. The final room upstairs was Ben's. The door was open, so she went inside. It wasn't like she hadn't been in there before—though she hadn't been looking at photos, for sure. She checked all the ones hanging on the wall, then the ones placed about the room on the bureau and the dresser. There was a gorgeous photo of Ben with his parents when he'd been maybe five or six.

"Reyna!"

She jumped as if he'd caught her snooping. "Coming!"

He waited at the bottom of the stairs.

"Did you find him?" She hurried down, hopeful that Ward was home and okay.

Ben shook his head. "His phone goes straight to voice mail now, and so does Mom's. I tried her house phone too, and she's not picking up."

"Should we drive over?"

"The sheriff is going to drive by. If she's avoiding the two of us, it won't do me any good to go over there. Maybe if our poking around in the past is the issue, she'll respond to the sheriff."

Reyna frowned at the idea. "I really hope my being here and doing the research I'm doing hasn't upset your family." She rolled her eyes and gave herself a mental kick. "Well, that was a ridiculous statement. How could it not?"

"Reyna." He took her by the hand and pulled her down

to sit on the third step with him. "Pops wanted this. He wanted you to help him find what no one else had—actual answers. I, unknown to him, was starting my own dig into the past. So nothing you've done has caused anything that wasn't already going to happen."

She felt a bit of relief at his words. The thought that she might have disturbed so many lives wasn't an easy one to swallow. But he made sense. Still, there was that nagging question of who had reacted in such an extreme manner, with her damaged tire, the fire and that note. The answer might prove more painful than the not knowing.

The fact that Eudora had warned her about the Widows was eye-opening. Would they have hidden the truth all these years? Sadly, it seemed all too possible.

"Thanks. That makes me feel a lot better about my part in this." Another frown tugged at her brow. "What did the sheriff say about Ward still not being home?"

"He's a grown man with no known health issues, so we have to wait twenty-four hours. If he doesn't show by then, she can officially get involved. Driving by my mom's house is a simpler issue. It falls under a welfare check. Not that Mom would appreciate the gesture."

Reyna laughed. "I'm sure she would not. But it's the thought that counts."

He braced his elbows on his knees, hands between his legs, and turned to her, putting them almost nose to nose. Reyna smiled. She really, really liked his eyes. His face. The rest of him.

"What're you thinking?" He shrugged half-heartedly. "About all this, I mean."

Focus back on the research, Reyna.

"I think that a lot of people know a little something. Maybe each one believes their particular fragment doesn't matter in the grand scheme of things. But if we can get them talking openly, we might make some headway. In any puzzle, every little piece matters."

"What about the fire and your tire and that warning?" He shook his head. "I swear I've never known folks around here to be so bullheaded."

"The unknown is scary. Change is scary to some." Reyna considered the people she had met. "Sometimes it's easier to stick with the known, with the routine. Then you don't have to wonder what will happen if anything or everything changes."

He held her gaze for a long time before he finally responded. "You're right. For a year now, I've been pretending what happened between me and my ex-fiancée didn't matter. Was no big deal. But it did matter, and it was a big deal. But I'm okay with that. I'm beyond it—have been, actually. The trouble was I was holding myself back."

They had talked last night about prior relationships. Reyna had confessed to never having had a serious one. And though Ben had been engaged, he had realized over the past year that what he'd felt had not been the deep kind of love he'd hoped for. He'd been reluctant to try again.

"I was afraid, as you say," he admitted now, "of what moving on might look like." He laughed softly. "But now I know exactly what I want looks like, and I can't wait to see more."

Her heart nearly stopped as the meaning of his heartfelt words sank in. "I'm right there with you. Ready to see what could happen next."

Reyna watched him closing that tiny distance between them, felt his lips press against hers. Smiling, she closed her eyes and melted into the kiss.

His fingers forked into her hair. Reyna rested her forehead against his face. The feel of his afternoon stubble and the ridges and planes of his handsome face had tingles firing through her.

A knock on the door had them jumping apart.

Ben shot up to answer it. Reyna took a breath and a little more time getting up. She braced a hand on the newel-post since her head was still spinning.

"Sheriff Norwood."

Beyond Ben's shoulder, Reyna spotted the sheriff at the door. Her heart took a dive, and she hurried to join him.

"Is everything okay?" he asked.

"Maybe," Norwood said with a glance around the yard and driveway. "You mind if I come in for a minute?"

"Course not." Ben opened the door wider. "Come on in."

Reyna hoped this was not going to be worse news.

"I stopped by Lucinda's house, and there was no answer."

"I appreciate you stopping by," Ben assured her. "She may have gone to the city for a day of shopping. She doesn't always keep me up to speed on her agenda, but with what's been happening, I can't help but worry. She's not answering my calls."

Norwood nodded. "I get it, and I've got a bad feeling you have cause to worry."

There was a new development. Her voice told the tale. "What's happened?" Reyna asked.

"The fire marshal has determined that the fire at the Jewel was not an accident. The way the candle burned told him that it had been lying horizontal from the moment it was lit. So whoever lit that candle wanted it to turn into a fire."

Reyna shook her head. "Wouldn't it have been easier to just take my laptop and other stuff?"

"I'm with you," Norwood agreed. "Which tells me this wasn't really about your stuff. It was about sending you a message."

"So the note left on my truck windshield wasn't some sort of prank," Ben suggested. "It was another message, like the fire but not as aggressive. Don't criminals usually escalate?"

"It doesn't make sense, for sure," Norwood said, "but there was a point—and that point was to scare you off." The last she directed at Reyna. "The fire was set during a time when no one was around to be hurt and in the middle of the day so it was more likely someone would see the trouble and call for help. It's as if the person or persons sending these messages weren't actually trying to hurt anyone. Even the damage to your tire was not created for optimal potential damage."

"Which suggests our perpetrator," Reyna offered, "is either not a seasoned criminal or not someone who really wants to make me disappear altogether."

"That's my thinking," Norwood agreed. "Whoever it is just wants you to stop digging around in the past. That said," she added, "desperation could change what we're seeing. We have to view this as a dangerous situation."

"Have you talked to Birdie?" Reyna hoped this didn't mean she wasn't safe at the bed-and-breakfast. A thread of fear worked its way through her at the reality of what they were talking about. As strong as she wanted to believe she was, she was not a fool.

"I have, and she took it in stride," Norwood said. "Since she doesn't have any guests right now, she has agreed to keep the doors locked as a precaution."

"I can't help feeling like this is all the more reason to be worried about where my grandfather is," Ben admitted.

"I've looked up his vehicle registration info—I'll have my deputies keeping an eye out for it. You check in with me in the morning, and if he's not back or hasn't called, we'll get the ball rolling on an alert."

Ben thanked her again as she left. He closed the door and turned back to Reyna. "You mind taking a ride with me? I'd like to do a little follow-up for myself before it gets dark."

"Let me get my bag."

6:00 p.m.

FOR A WHILE, they didn't speak, just rode. Reyna was okay with that. She needed to think. To sort through the details that wouldn't quite gel.

"The way I see it," she said when he'd cruised down the next street, "we have two prime suspects—Walls and Landon. Both appeared to have some sort of issue with one of the Three."

She opted not to mention the Widows. They both knew they were suspects as well, but Reyna wasn't ready to go there until absolutely necessary. It was better to allow the possibility to evolve naturally. That way, Ben could come to the conclusion himself.

Ben made a turn back onto Main Street. "No one has ever mentioned trouble with Coach Landon beyond the disagreement at the reunion," he reminded her. "Likewise, most folks believe Walls is a good man who wouldn't have bothered with revenge." He lifted one shoulder in a half-hearted shrug. "But who really knows what a person is capable of if backed into a corner—even one of their own making."

"Being on the team was significant in the lives of the

Three," she pointed out. "To school kids, particularly in the high school years, being a part of a team is a big deal. The fact that those jerseys were hanging in that cabin with the rest of the stuff in what was obviously a shrine to their memories confirms as much."

Ben slowed as they passed the Jewel. Reyna wished she could find the truth—before it was too late for Eudora. Birdie would be relieved if for no other reason than it would allow the woman she loved so much to slip into the depths of her horrible disease with some semblance of peace.

"If only," Reyna said, her gaze floating over the lovely homes along Main Street, "the secret keeper would give us a clue."

"I think there's a vow that precludes that possibility." Ben pulled into the Shop and Save Market parking lot, turned around and headed back along Main Street in the other direction.

Reyna laughed. "Or there's a blackmailable reason the secret keeper is afraid to come forward."

"That too," he agreed.

They drove past the homes of the Widows, checked the Henry place and found no sign of anyone, including Ward. How did one man disappear so completely in such a small town?

The shock at her own question resonated profoundly through Reyna.

How had three men disappeared so completely from this little town?

Someone had to know something. The trouble was in finding that someone and prompting him or her to talk about the something.

"Before we call it a night," she said, breaking the silence that had fallen between them, "let's stop by to see Coach

Landon again. I want to ask him straight up what happened between him and Duke Fuller over Jesse Carson."

"He may not be willing to answer," Ben pointed out.

"But unless he's very good at the poker-face thing, we will get a reaction, particularly when we mention talking to Jesse just today. I'd like to see that reaction."

Ben glanced at her. "Now that you mention it, I'd kind of like to see that myself."

He turned left at the next intersection, drove around the block and headed back into town. Reyna did some research on her cell while he drove. She searched for more information on Landon and on Duke Fuller. She had already seen everything that populated the results, so she moved on to the Carson family. The typical social media hits about Jesse. Then she searched the name *Father Vincent Cullen*, the priest who had officiated at the memorial service for the Three when they'd finally been declared dead.

There were a good many hits, but none were the priest who lived in Whispering Winds—who had lived here for more than sixty years. She checked the church's website. Found no mention of him.

How strange was that? Other than the church website, she hadn't actually expected to find him on any sort of social media. He hadn't seemed the type. But she had expected newspaper mentions and that sort of thing. Just because he didn't do social media didn't mean he didn't get mentioned by other people.

But there was nothing.

Not a single mention.

Strange.

"You want me to go to the door? Or do you want to go together?"

Reyna jumped. She'd been so deep in thought she hadn't realized they had arrived at Landon's home.

"We're in this together."

Ben flashed her the kind of smile that reminded her that finishing this project was not going to be an easy wrap.

They climbed out of the truck and made their way up the sidewalk. She considered mentioning the oddity of finding nothing about the priest on the internet but then decided it was better to ask the priest personally and see his reaction. No need to suggest the local priest was on her list of potential suspects until she had something more than a lack of hits on the net.

Ben knocked on Landon's door, and they waited. There was no sound inside. No lights, and it was getting dark now. There should have been lights on inside.

Another knock. Then the seemingly endless minutes that crept by without a response. Reyna surveyed the block. A little on the shabby side, but nothing out of the ordinary. No dogs barking. No neighbors peeking beyond curtains.

Ben knocked a third time, and when no answer came, he gestured to his truck. "I suppose we can go. He is evidently out."

"Guess so. Let's take a ride past the church. See if Father Cullen is home."

"Maybe he's the keeper of secrets," Ben said.

Made sense to Reyna. He supposedly knew everything.

But Father Cullen wasn't home either. How was it that every single person they wanted to see was suddenly missing?

Reyna had a sneaking suspicion that all those secrets were building toward a crescendo.

The ride back to the Kane home was quiet—too quiet. Ben was worried, and his worry was only mounting. Reyna had to admit that all these folks ducking them and the little threats were worrisome. But none of it troubled her the way his missing grandfather did.

Once in the house, Ben did a walk-through—no matter that his grandfather's truck was not in the driveway.

Reyna figured they could both use some coffee. Maybe talking out the day's events would help one or both.

The scent of fresh-brewed coffee had just started to fill the kitchen when Ben came into the room.

"We need to look this up." He showed her a prescription medicine bottle for Ward Kane. Obviously he'd been prowling the man's room.

Reyna took the bottle from him and went to the table where she'd left her cell. She typed in the name of the drug. The words on the screen split through her with a vengeance. Her gaze connected with his. "It's primarily used in the treatment of Parkinson's disease."

The shock on his face made her chest tighten.

Reyna checked the details on the label—prescribed just weeks ago.

"I've known a number of people with this," she said, understanding what he was thinking. "It's not fatal. Not the way most people think. It can contribute to a shortened life span, but there are medications like this one that can help control the symptoms."

The words sounded hollow even to her. Good grief, his grandfather was eighty-five. Clearly this was not a good thing for his life expectancy.

"Have you noticed any symptoms?" she asked. "Tremors? Trouble walking? Any psychosis?" She hadn't noticed any of those things in Ward, but frankly she hadn't seen that much of him. This was the very last thing Ben needed on top of the deep dig into his father's disappearance. If Reyna hadn't felt bad already for barging into his life, she did now.

"I should tell the sheriff about this."

The defeat in his voice, in his eyes, tugged at her heart. "You should," she agreed.

Was this why Ward had wanted to help Reyna find answers? Because he feared his days were numbered more so than before?

But all she'd managed to do so far was find more questions.

Chapter Twelve

Friday, April 26, 7:30 a.m.

Ben walked around the house, scanned the property for as far as he could see. His grandfather was still MIA.

Where in the world was he?

And why hadn't he told Ben that he was sick?

Ben set his hands on his hips and exhaled a big breath. Ward Kane had always been steady, easygoing. Never a hothead or one to go off on a tangent. This was so, so wrong. It was possible the illness—if he and Reyna were right about the Parkinson's—had caused him not to behave in his usual manner. Ben had lain in bed last night and gone over every minute with his grandfather over the past few weeks. He hadn't noticed any unusual symptoms. Yeah, he had a bit of a tremor, but the man was eighty-five—was that so unusual? He got around great, in Ben's opinion, for a man of his age. If there were other things going on, he'd kept them well hidden.

Then there was his sudden interest in poking around in the disappearance of his only son. For all his adult life, Ben had assumed that his mother and grandfather had come to terms with what had happened and chosen not to look back.

Had this diagnosis prompted a sudden urgency to find the truth?

Ben couldn't deny that deep down he'd considered wanting the same closure. Who wouldn't?

But wanting it and going after it were two very different things. Other people were involved, and not everyone wanted to stir the hornet's nest.

The question, in his mind, was *Why?* Who would be opposed to finding the truth? There was no reason, unless there was some sort of guilt. Ben hated the idea that someone in this town—maybe someone he encountered regularly or considered a friend—might have been involved in his father going missing.

Murder.

His father hadn't just gone missing; he'd likely been murdered.

Ben stared at the ground a moment. All these years he and his mother—his grandfather too—had tiptoed around the idea. They'd skirted the possibility without acknowledging or accepting it. Never allowed themselves to dwell on the idea that JR Ward had been murdered—that all three of the missing men had been murdered.

Alien abduction, escape to some tropical island, all the other options were easier to consider.

It was time to face the fact that none of those things were true. His father was dead. His friends were dead. And someone had murdered them.

That someone was still out there—assuming he hadn't died in the past thirty years—living his life.

Unless it was a *she.*

Ben thought of his mother and how Eudora had said she knew what she was up to. She'd thought she was talking to JR. Had Eudora meant that Gordon Walls was a threat because Lucinda had cheated on him with JR? She'd also said Reyna should be worried about the Widows. The Widows had been considered suspects in the beginning. They were the wives, after all. Whenever a spouse disappeared, the other half of the couple was the primary suspect. But what reason would his mother have had to kill his father? Ben had no memory of arguments or unhappiness. Their family photos showed no hint of dissension.

Surely his grandfather would have been aware of any issues between JR and Lucinda.

Ben walked back toward the house. His heart felt heavy and his mind was going in a dozen directions at once.

"It's always best to have coffee before thinking so deeply."

Ben turned to see Reyna on the porch, where she held two mugs.

He smiled, liked the way she looked in the mornings. The nightshirt Birdie had lent her was a little loose but fell against her thighs in just the right spot… It made his mouth dry. Her hair was a fiery mass of waves and maybe a few tangles. As much as he enjoyed their lovemaking, just having her next to him last night had felt comfortable…right. He hadn't felt that kind of ease with anyone in a long time. Not even his ex-fiancée. There had always been a tension or uncertainty between them. As if they'd almost fit but not quite.

"Thanks. I meant to get back in there and pour a cup, but I never made it."

He joined her on the porch, where she'd taken a seat on the top step. "He's still not home."

Ben stared into his mug of dark brew. "No." He turned to her. "I'm seriously worried about him, Reyna. This is way, way out of character. He never just takes off like this."

"Could be the disease."

He nodded. "Could be."

"I say," Reyna offered, "that we grab a piece of toast and head for your mom's house. Maybe stop by the Henry place. See if he's shown up at either place. We can check in with Sheriff Norwood, see if her search has found anyone who's seen him."

"That's a good plan." Tracking down his grandfather wasn't exactly part of Reyna's work here, but he appreciated her offer to help. He'd never been bothered about doing things alone, but somehow this was different. He was pretty sure that if she wasn't around he would be lonely.

He had no idea how he would remedy that issue when she was gone.

"Have you ever—" he stood, offered her his hand "—had toast with peanut butter for breakfast?"

She took his hand, and he pulled her to her feet. "I can't say that I have."

"A little protein goes a long way when you have stuff to do."

Henry Property
Shadow Brook Lane
9:00 a.m.

REYNA CLIMBED OUT of the truck and met Ben at the hood. The house looked as abandoned as it had the last time they'd stopped by. The disappointment on his face warned that his worry was escalating.

"We can walk through," he said, "though I don't expect that anything's changed."

"We're here." Reyna tried to sound chipper. "Might as well."

A methodical walk-through of the old house revealed nothing but dust and the tools Ben had left on-site. The doors had still been locked. From there, they exited through the back door and went from one outbuilding to the other. Nothing disturbed. If Ward had been here, he hadn't taken anything or left anything behind.

On the way back to the truck, Reyna asked, "We headed to your mom's house next?"

He nodded. "I tried calling her first thing this morning, and the call went straight to voice mail again."

Reyna didn't bother mentioning that his mother could have lost her phone or forgotten to charge it. None of those things were likely true, but they sounded logical. Whatever was going on, the rest of Ben's family had fallen off the radar.

Kane Residence
Thistle Lane
9:45 a.m.

REYNA UNDERSTOOD BEFORE they emerged from Ben's truck that nothing had changed here either. Her instincts were humming, and not in a good way.

This time after he knocked a couple of times, Ben tried the door. It opened.

He exchanged a look with Reyna, and the worry she'd been watching escalate all morning morphed into something closer to fear.

"Mom?" he called out as they entered the front hall.

No scent of morning coffee…no smells of prepared

foods. Nothing that suggested someone had been up and around doing anything at all.

Reyna's nerves were jumping. This was not good. Ben moved forward, heading for the kitchen. She ventured into the parlor, where they'd met with Lucinda just a few days before.

The photo albums they'd looked at were no longer stacked in neat rows on the coffee table but were scattered about. Some on the table, some on the sofa. A couple open. Reyna sat down and picked up the first of the two open albums. This one was in the couple's younger days. There were numerous photos of JR during high school. Several of him with Duke Fuller and Judson Evans. They were all smiling widely, their lives just beginning to evolve into what had come next.

Reyna set the album aside and picked up the other one that had been left open. The photos were mostly from just before the Three's disappearance. Taking her time, she moved through the images slowly, examining each one with a close eye. What had these men been thinking in the weeks and months before they'd just vanished?

Had there been marital problems? No one seemed to believe so.

Financial problems? None had been found.

There was the fact that Lucinda had dumped Gordon Walls for JR Kane, but that had been more than seven years earlier.

Then there was the disagreement over Jesse Carson between Duke Fuller and Coach Landon. Why would Fuller care if his former teammate's kid played on the team, was the coach's new chosen one?

Reyna paused on a photo of the Three. JR and Judson were goofing around, but Duke was sort of off to himself.

His expression appeared brooding. Reyna turned back and looked for instances of a similar scene—one with Duke Fuller looking sullen and separate from the others.

There were plenty of others. Rey's pulse sped up. In those final weeks before they'd disappeared, Duke looked as if he'd had the weight of the world on his shoulders and even his friends couldn't help him. Reyna set the album aside and reached for the one from their high school days. She studied the photos carefully. In all the team photos Duke looked distracted. Not really unhappy, just not as exuberant as his friends.

"Her car is in the garage," Ben said from the doorway.

She'd been so engrossed in the photos and what this thing plaguing Fuller might've meant that she hadn't heard Ben come into the room.

Reyna stood. "Did you check upstairs?"

Their gazes locked and held for a long moment.

He shook his head. "I'll do that now."

If his mother had fallen ill…

"Not going there," Reyna muttered. She reached for the album, and it slid onto the floor. "Dang it." She crouched down to pick it up, but something beneath the sofa snagged her attention. She leaned down to get a better look. The sofa was one of the higher-legged ones, so it wasn't difficult to see beneath it.

A cell phone lay face down on the floor.

Oh, no.

Reyna reached for it, turned it over and touched the screen to awaken it.

Dozens of missed calls from Ben.

This was his mother's cell phone.

"Ben!" The phone gripped in her hand, she hurried to

the hall. He was already coming down the stairs. Reyna held up the phone. “This was under the sofa.”

Ben took the phone and checked the screen. He nodded. “It’s hers. I don’t know her passcode, so I can’t get past the lock screen.”

The notifications had allowed Reyna to see there were missed calls from Ben, but now that those had cleared, they couldn’t see anything else without the passcode.

But what was glaringly obvious was that Lucinda Kane had left her house without her car or her phone.

Cold slinking through her, Reyna dared to ask, “Did you find her handbag?”

“I didn’t notice one sitting around in her room.”

“Where does she enter the house most frequently? The front or the back?”

“The back.”

Reyna led the way through the front hall and into the kitchen. The rack over the bench by the back door held a sweater, a raincoat and a taupe-colored handbag. Reyna’s gut clenched.

“Do you want to check for her wallet? See if that’s the handbag she’s been carrying most recently?” Most women changed handbags fairly often. The essentials would be in the one she was currently using.

Ben opened the bag and withdrew her wallet. He looked to Reyna. “This can’t be right. Whatever Sheriff Norwood believes, something is going on, and it involves my grandfather and my mother.”

“You’re right.” Reyna glanced around the kitchen to give herself a moment to think before she spoke. “We should check the other widows’ houses before we call the sheriff. If they’re all three missing, that means something different from just your mom and your grandfather being MIA."

He tucked the wallet back into his mother's bag. "I'm locking up. I don't want to leave the house open like this."

"You have a key in case you need to get back in?"

He nodded. "Let's go."

Evans Residence
Blackberry Trail
11:00 a.m.

BEN PARKED NEXT to Harlowe Evans's car. It had been sitting in that same spot the last time he and Reyna had come over.

"We should try the door if she doesn't answer," Reyna suggested.

"Yeah."

They got out together and headed for the porch. It was too quiet. He already had this gut feeling that no one was home.

He knocked. "I hate to even say this out loud." Since no one answered the door and it remained quiet inside, he knocked again. "But if she's not here and then we go to Ms. Fuller's house and find the same situation…"

"That will be eerie, and let's not even go there until we have to. One step at a time."

After a third knock with no answer, Ben tried the door. It opened.

"You want me to go inside? I'm not from around here," Reyna offered. "The sheriff might cut me some slack for trespassing."

"We go together."

Again, inside there were no scents that suggested any sort of food or beverage prep had taken place that morning. The house was neat. And it was a clear shot from the front to the back considering the renovations that had been done. The wide-open first floor showed no sign of the owner's presence.

The drop zone for coats and shoes was next to the front door, and Ms. Evans's handbag hung next to a lightweight jacket. This time Ben preferred that Reyna did the honors. She unzipped the bag and spotted the woman's wallet.

"Try her cell number," Reyna suggested.

Ben withdrew his phone, scrolled his contacts until he found her name and tapped. Seconds later the muffled sound of the phone ringing came from the other side of the room. He followed the sound, found the phone on the island partially concealed by a tea towel.

The top notification visible was a missed called from a number not in the woman's contacts.

"You recognize this number?" Reyna asked, showing him the screen.

He entered the number into his screen, and Sheriff Norwood's name appeared. He ended the call.

Norwood had tried to reach all three of the Widows. The only reason her number hadn't been the top notification on Ben's mom's phone was because of his calls.

There was a passcode, so that was all they were getting from the phone. He placed it back on the counter.

"I'll take a walk-through upstairs," he said, heading for the staircase.

"I'll look around down here."

Being in his mother's house hadn't felt so strange because she was family. But this was different. If Ms. Evans walked in right now and caught them snooping around, she would likely not be happy. Not that Ben could blame her. And their only excuse would probably not make her feel any better.

While Ben had a look upstairs, Reyna explored downstairs. There were no photos or albums lying around. The entire downstairs was neat, everything in its place. Reyna thought about the note she'd gotten the other night, the one stuck on Ben's truck windshield. She checked through the cabinets in the island and near the sink until she found the one where the trash bin was tucked. Like the rest of the place, even the trash smelled clean. There was very little in the bin.

At the bottom, beneath a discarded potato chip bag and an empty cookie bag, were newspaper clippings. Reyna clawed them up from the bottom of the bin and spread them across the counter.

These weren't new clippings—these were from decades ago. Most were about the search for the missing men. But one was about the fundraiser being held at Our Lady of the Mountain Church. Reyna smoothed the crumpled article. A photo of the football team, the Three included, was front and center. Father Cullen was huddled close to one of the players, so close you could hardly see his face.

The difference between the article about the fundraiser at the church and the others was that Harlowe Evans had crumpled this one. Reyna read the article and found nothing that set off alarm bells. It was fairly cut-and-dried—the team had made the playoffs and extra funds were needed for travel, thus the fundraiser.

"You find anything?" Ben came up beside her.

"Just these clippings in the trash."

He surveyed the articles, then shook his head. "Whatever is going on, it doesn't feel like these women left voluntarily."

"We should check the Fuller home and call Sheriff Norwood."

If the women had been missing since yesterday…they could be running out of time.

Chapter Thirteen

Fuller Residence
Hawk's Way
11:45 a.m.

There was no answer at the Fuller house either, but the door was locked. A walk around the property showed the owner's car was not home. The detached garage had windows, so they could see inside. Ben had checked the one other larger building just in case the car was in there. It was not.

"So maybe we've overreacted," Reyna offered. "The three of them could have taken a trip somewhere. A shopping spree or a spa getaway." She shrugged. "Girl trip."

"Except," he countered, "why would my mom and Ms. Evans leave their phones at home? Leave their houses unlocked?"

Reyna put her hands up. "You got me there."

Ben thought for a moment about what he wanted to do. It might not have been the smartest step, but his curiosity was getting the better of him. He really needed to see if Ms. Fuller was inside the house—car or no car. And whether her phone was in there.

"I think I'll check a few windows. If there's one unlocked I'm going inside to check things out. You let me know if company arrives."

"I'm sure there are things I should say to you right now," Reyna pointed out. "Like the fact that breaking and entering is a crime."

"I promise I won't break anything." He shot her a grin, and she just shook her head. "Keeping watch."

She sat down in the glider on the porch and gestured for him to carry on.

Ben started with the windows on the porch. The home's windows were double hung with sliding screens that made the task far easier. All four front windows on the first level were locked. He moved all the way around the house until, next to the back door, he found the one he needed. The screen slid up out of the way, and the window sash followed. Not a very big window, but he felt confident he could work his way through.

He pulled his upper body into the opening and reached for the floor. Once he'd braced his hands there, he pulled his lower torso and legs through. He closed the window and locked it just to make sure no one else did the same.

The laundry room, where he'd entered, led into the kitchen. He checked around the room, remembered to look in the garbage can before moving on. Reyna had found newspaper clippings in Ms. Evans's trash.

The entire first floor was in order, and there was no sign of the owner, her cell phone or a handbag. He called her cell to ensure it was not in the house. If it was, it had either been silenced or the battery had died and it no longer rang. He moved on to the upstairs, where he found the same. No Deidre Fuller.

As he approached the front door to join Reyna on the porch, it occurred to him that none of the security systems in the houses had been armed. He stared at the keypad next to the front door.

He was surprised this one hadn't been.

He couldn't exit via the front door since the dead bolt was the kind that needed a key to engage or disengage. The back door, on the other hand, had no dead bolt. When he had exited via that back door, locking it behind him, and reached the front of the house, Reyna looked to him for an update.

He sat down next to her. "No handbag. No cell phone. No sign of the owner."

"Time to call the sheriff," she suggested.

Ben nodded and reached for his phone. He put through the call and relayed all the details they'd discovered—except for the part about him going into Ms. Fuller's locked house. He left it at *no answer and no car.*

When he'd hung up, he passed along the sheriff's response. "She's sending deputies to check the Kane and Evans homes for any signs of forced entry or a struggle—which we know she won't find. That's about all she can do at this point."

"What do you think we should do now?" Reyna asked. "We can't just sit around and wait to see who disappears next."

She was right about that. They had to do something.

"We can go back to see the priest." Ben shrugged. "Maybe he's home now. If so, we tell him what's going on. Maybe if he knows anything at all he'll toss us a bone. Anything to give us a direction to go."

"Unless he's the one hiding the most secrets."

Ben considered the probability that many priests knew plenty of secrets about their parishioners. Secrets they could never share with anyone.

"Then I guess we've kind of hit a brick wall." Where

on earth were his mother and his grandfather? This was all kinds of crazy.

"Back when I was writing fiction," she said, "I developed a number of sources in areas where I might need to do research. One of them was a retired FBI agent. I emailed him about Father Cullen. I know it might seem a reach, but the fact that when I did some digging on the net I couldn't find anything about him feels off. Scrubbing your history from cyberspace is not an easy feat. I didn't mention this before because maybe it's nothing, but I don't want to ignore even the most unlikely possibility. In any event, I hope to hear back from him later today."

Ben shook his head and laughed out loud. "This is just a small town in Tennessee—how can we have all these unsolved mysteries?"

And missing people?

"Let's go see the priest." Reyna stood, grabbed him by the hand and pulled him to his feet. "Who knows—maybe we'll hear from the sheriff or my FBI contact by the time we've interviewed the priest again, assuming he's home."

He had a feeling that was wishful thinking.

Our Lady of the Mountain
Kings Lane
1:00 p.m.

LIKE EVERY DOOR they'd knocked on so far today, there was no answer at the rectory.

Reyna wasn't one to easily admit defeat, but this was getting ridiculous. Where the hell was everyone?

"Maybe he's in the church," she suggested. "If not, the current priest might know where he is."

"Could be out for a walk," Ben said as they took the

cobblestone path that led back to the parking area. "It's a nice day. I've seen him out walking before."

"Or maybe at lunch." Reyna's stomach had already reminded her that they hadn't stopped long enough to grab a bite.

Ben grinned. "We should do that before our next stop."

"You won't get any argument from me."

Father Garrett Jordan had just exited the church and was coming down the steps when they reached the front of the building. He sucked on a cigarette and released a puff of smoke.

"Afternoon, Father," Ben said, announcing their presence since the man hadn't spotted them.

"Good afternoon to you." The priest smiled and waved the smoke in his hand. "A bad habit I've never been able to kick."

Reyna returned his smile. "We all have one kind or the other." She offered her hand as he reached the bottom step. "Reyna Hart. Father Cullen may have told you I'm here researching the Three."

He gave a nod. "Several dedicated parishioners have reported your activities, Ms. Hart—Father Cullen included."

She laughed. "It's a small town," she agreed. "The news of a stranger picking through the past travels quickly."

"Indeed." He looked from Reyna to Ben and back. "How can I help you today?"

"We don't want to hold you up," Ben said, "if you were on your way out."

"Off to lunch at the diner. Nothing that can't wait."

Garrett Jordan wasn't much older than Ben, Reyna decided. Fortyish, maybe.

"We hoped to speak with Father Cullen again," she said. "But he's out. Do you know when he might return?"

Jordan's brows drew together. "I haven't seen him today. Yesterday either, for that matter. When last we spoke he seemed distressed over the stir about the past." He smiled at Reyna. "He's never talked about it very much. My impression is that he feels he failed those three young men. As we get older we tend to reflect on the mistakes—or those things we perceive as mistakes—we've made. Father Cullen is looking back a great deal lately."

"When you see him, Father," Ben said, "can you let him know we'd like to speak with him again? It's very important."

Jordan gave a slow nod and appeared to struggle a bit with himself before responding. "I feel I should share something with you that will perhaps give you some insight into Father Cullen's current situation. He's not been himself for a bit. You see, he has a brain tumor. Sadly, it's inoperable, and it's only a matter of time before he will be leaving us. It's not common knowledge, but I hope you might be able to make your judgments a bit more accurately knowing this."

"I'm so sorry to hear that." Reyna looked to Ben, uncertain what else to say. Good grief, they'd found the prescription in his grandfather's room, and now this. It was true that all those who might've known details about the Three and their disappearance were going fast.

"Thanks for letting us know, Father," Ben said. "It's a shame. He's an institution in this town."

"A hard act to follow, for sure," Jordan said. "As for catching him, generally if he's out for a walk or lunch, he comes back fairly quickly. Feel free to wait for him. He never locks his door."

"We'll do that," Ben said. "Enjoy your lunch. We'll be heading that way next."

Father Jordan gave another nod and hurried to his car. He tucked his half-smoked cigarette into his mouth and climbed in and drove away.

"Wow." Reyna turned to Ben. "Eudora and your grandfather are right. We're running out of time."

"That's what worries me," he admitted. He hitched his head toward the cobblestone path that led to the rectory. "The father said we could wait."

"He did," she agreed.

As Father Jordan had said, the door to the rectory was unlocked.

"Father Cullen?" Reyna called out as they entered.

No answer, of course.

Rather than have a seat and wait, they wandered around the space. Looking but not touching. Ben checked the bedroom to ensure Cullen wasn't napping.

She perused the few framed photos and the notes lying around for anything related to the Three.

Her cell vibrated, and Reyna dug it free of her pocket. It was Jimmy Corbin. She accepted the call from her FBI research source and said, "Hey."

"Hey, Reyna. Got your email last night, and I was intrigued. You're right. It's not easy removing your history so thoroughly. So I checked into your priest, Cullen."

Reyna stilled, waited for the news that might very well point them in the right direction. He wouldn't have responded by phone if he'd found nothing.

"There's not a lot I can tell you because it's classified."

Classified? There was an answer she hadn't seen coming. "Okay."

"What I can say is that if there's trouble with this guy… it might be more than a little dangerous, so I'd steer clear if possible. And," he said, "if something is going on, we probably need to know about it. So keep me posted but give this man a wide berth. You got it?"

"Got it. Thanks, Jimmy. I'll let you know if this gets hairy."

"Good, and if you get back up to New York," he said, "let me know. We can do lunch and catch up."

"That would be nice," she agreed. "Maybe one day soon."

When the call ended, Ben looked at her expectantly.

"He couldn't tell me a lot about Cullen." She glanced around the room. "But it sounds like this man is not who we think he is, and…we should be careful because his past… It could be dangerous to anyone poking around."

Ben made a face. "Are you serious?"

"Yeah." Reyna glanced around the room. "I'm not sure how this helps us in what we're looking for."

"Unless whatever trouble revolving around him struck thirty years ago."

"I guess that's possible," she admitted.

Ben shook his head. "I'm sure your source knows what he's talking about, but honestly I can't see Father Cullen making anyone disappear."

The wiliest killers were the ones you didn't see coming. Besides, based on what Jimmy had said, this priest could be in witness protection. Maybe he'd ratted out a mob boss or something.

"We hanging around here for a while longer?" She didn't really see the point. If he reappeared, he wasn't going to tell them anything they didn't already know, particularly if it implicated him and his past somehow.

Ben showed her a photo he'd taken with his phone. "This is hanging on the lamp next to his bed. It looks familiar, but I can't place it."

It was a cross on a silver chain. The cross was small and rustic. Not your typical polished-with-smooth-edges silver cross. It looked handmade, primitive. Like ancient nails or little daggers held together by small lengths of barbed wire.

"I don't recognize it, but I'm glad you snapped a pic in case we figure it out later."

Reyna took one more lingering look around. "I suppose there's nothing left to do except..." She turned to Ben. "Do you think we could go back to the cabin?"

"We'd have to get permission from Sheriff Norwood." He nodded. "But I'd like to see it again too."

"Let's give it a shot, then."

Trout Lake
2:00 p.m.

THEY'D GRABBED BURGERS, fries and drinks from the diner on the way to the Fuller lake property. Reyna hadn't realized how hungry she'd been until she'd smelled those fries. She also hadn't eaten so fast since she'd been a kid.

By the time they were parked, she was ready to walk off those couple thousand or so calories. Norwood had said that her head forensic guy, Sergeant David Snelling, might still be there wrapping things up, and as long as they didn't get in his way, they could look around. They'd been there before, so it wasn't like they were new to the scene. Their prints would already be there. Maybe hairs or other clothing fibers too.

Snelling was gone when they reached the cabin. Crime scene tape was still draped around the place. They walked around to the back and checked out the holes left from digging up the area where the three wooden crosses had been.

The smell of freshly turned earth hung in the air. The three crosses were gone—taken in as evidence, she supposed. They walked around the entire exterior before ducking under the tape and going to the door.

A warning that the cabin was a crime scene had been posted on the door.

"She didn't say we couldn't go in," Ben pointed out.

"She did not," Reyna agreed.

He opened the door, and they walked inside. The gloom had them pulling out their cell phones and turning on the flashlight apps. Reyna walked around the room slowly, surveying every photo on the wall again, examining each closely for anything she might have missed before. When she reached another photo that showed Duke Fuller standing apart from the others and looking distant or upset, she turned to Ben. He was examining the jerseys hanging on the wall as closely as she had been the photos. She wondered if the idea that his father had worn that jersey was tearing at him inside.

"Hey." When he glanced her way, she went on. "This is another example of the Duke thing I was telling you about."

He walked over to join her.

"See how he's standing back and he looks upset or distracted?"

"I do," he said. "There was something going on with him, don't you think?"

"But unless he shared whatever it was with someone besides his two best friends, we may never know what it was."

Ben leaned closer to the photo. "Is he wearing a chain?" He touched his own throat.

Reyna peered at the photo. “He is. Can’t tell what kind it is, but he’s definitely wearing something.”

As if mutual understanding that it could be the cross found in Father Cullen’s room hit them both at the same time, they moved from photo to photo that included Duke, looking for a better view of whatever sort of chain he wore.

“Got it,” Ben said.

Reyna hurried over to see. “That’s it.” She nodded. “I mean, it could just be one like it, but it’s definitely the same sort of cross.”

Their gazes met, and they both understood that was not the case. Neither of them had ever seen one anything like it.

“If that isn’t Duke Fuller’s cross and chain hanging in the priest’s room, then it’s one just like it.”

“Maybe the priest gave it to him,” Reyna offered. “He may have had one like it.”

“Do priests usually give teenage guys chains with crosses?”

She shrugged. “I don’t know. I guess we’ll have to ask him.”

“We should take this one with us.” Ben snagged the photo. “I’ll give it to Norwood when I see her again and tell her about the cross in Cullen’s room.”

“We should just find out where she is and go there now before something happens to the cross.”

Ben considered the idea, then nodded. “You’re right. If Cullen figures out we’ve been there, it could disappear.”

“After that,” Reyna said, “I think we should pay another visit to Coach Landon. Just to make sure he hasn’t disappeared too. Everybody else appears to have vanished.”

"Good idea."

As they drove back to town, Ben was just about to call Norwood when his cell sounded off. "Hey, Sheriff. I was just about to call you." He glanced at Reyna before turning his attention back to the highway.

Reyna hoped this was good news, but she had a bad, bad feeling it was not.

Her own cell started to vibrate in her pocket, and she tugged it out and answered. "This is Reyna."

"Reyna, it's Birdie. I'm so sorry to bother you, but I really need your help. Would you mind coming to the Jewel and helping me out?"

"Of course I will. Are you okay?"

"Well, it's a little embarrassing, but I was working in the yard all day, trying to get ahead of the weeds. I got all sweaty and dirty, so I decided to shower and, good Lord, I fell getting out. I'm so embarrassed. I'm as naked as the day I was born, and I can't even crawl to my room."

"Don't try to move. I'm on my way." Reyna ended the call and turned to Ben, who was just ending his own. "Everything okay?"

"I don't know. They found my grandfather's truck."

Dread slid through her veins as she waited for him to go on.

"He wasn't there. No sign of foul play."

Relief gushed along the same path the dread had taken. "That's good, right?"

"Hopefully." The worry etched in his profile warned he was far from sure about that. "I need to get over there." He glanced at her. "You were saying you'd be right there to someone."

Oh, no. "I'm sorry. Birdie needs me." Reyna felt torn about leaving Ben, but she certainly couldn't ignore the elderly woman. She may have broken something. "Do you mind just dropping me off there?"

"No problem. You take care of Birdie. I can handle this. I'll catch up with you as soon as I can."

"Okay."

She really hated that Ben had to do this alone. But Birdie needed help. How could Reyna say no?

Chapter Fourteen

The Jewel Bed & Breakfast
Main Street
3:55 p.m.

Reyna watched Ben drive away, and worry that she should have gone with him settled on her shoulders. The sheriff would be there, maybe other deputies with whom he was acquainted. He would be okay. She repeated this twice more.

Deep breath. Reyna started forward. Birdie needed her. She was alone, and she was elderly. She could be seriously injured.

Her cell vibrated in her pocket, and she pulled it free to check the screen. The Light Memory Care Center. Her heart sped up. Had Eudora taken another turn for the worse?

Barely able to get the word out, she said, "Hello."

"Reyna Hart?"

"Yes, this is she."

"Ms. Hart, I'm calling to see if you've heard from Ms. Davenport—she seems to have disappeared."

"What do you mean?" More worry joined the mix of fear already twisting in Reyna's belly.

"After lunch, when the therapist went to her room for her session, Eudora was gone. When we didn't find her anywhere on the first floor of the center, we checked the security footage. She was seen leaving the facility with an unidentified woman around one thirty."

"Was this woman not someone who works at the facility? I mean, I'm assuming you're saying she wasn't a registered visitor. So was she an employee?"

"We can't be sure. She was wearing a hoodie."

Oh dear God. "Have you called the authorities?" Who would take Eudora out of the facility? This was beyond inexplicable.

"We have. They're here now reviewing the security footage and questioning employees and patients. We hoped you might have heard from her since you visited her so often over the past few months. One of her nurses remembered you and we found your number in Eudora's bedside table. We hated to call but we haven't been able to reach her emergency contact, Birdie Jewel. Frankly, we're a little desperate."

A frown tugged at Reyna's brow. "I'm sorry, no. I haven't heard from her since we visited yesterday. But I'm at Ms. Jewel's home now. Unfortunately, she's had a fall." Reyna walked faster toward the entrance. "I'll check with her to see if there is anyone else we can call."

"If you hear from Eudora or learn any new information," the woman said, "please let us know."

"I will, of course. I can check with her friends here in Whispering Winds. If I learn anything, I will let you know that as well," Reyna assured her.

When the call ended, she reached for the door of the Jewel. It was locked. Oh, no. Sheriff Norwood had urged Birdie to keep the door locked. How was Reyna going to get inside?

Reyna called Birdie's phone.

"Are you here?" she asked without a hello.

"I am but the door is locked. Should I call 911?"

The call abruptly ended.

Reyna stared at the screen. "What the…?"

The sound of the locks releasing had Reyna shifting her attention to the door.

The door opened and Birdie stood there—fully clothed. She put her hand to her chest. "Thank goodness you're here."

Before Reyna could demand to know what was going on or consider telling her about Eudora, Birdie grabbed her by the arm and pulled her inside. Just as quickly, she closed and secured the door once more.

"What's going on?" The notion that Birdie had obviously lied to her had frustration bubbling over. The possibility that she could have taken Eudora from the facility suddenly seemed far too possible. No, Reyna decided. Not possible. Probable. "Birdie, have you—"

"Come with me," she interrupted. She grabbed Reyna and ushered her along with surprising strength and swiftness.

The elderly woman didn't stop until she'd reached a back room, a former rear parlor that she'd transformed into a library complete with hundreds, if not thousands, of books.

For a moment Reyna could only stare, certain she wasn't seeing what…she was obviously seeing. People were seated around the room on sofas and chairs. *Eudora.* Birdie had taken her from the center! Holy cow! Before she could demand to know what the meaning of all this was, Reyna's attention settled on the others present. Ward Kane! He was sitting right there as if his grandson and the sheriff weren't out looking for him.

The sound of the pocket doors clacking shut jerked Reyna from the disbelief. She turned to Birdie. "What is this?"

"I think you know everyone," Birdie said.

The Widows were here. The three of them sat together on a sofa. All three glanced at Reyna and smiled. Father Cullen sat in a chair on the far side of the room as if he had been speaking to or directing the group meeting.

Reyna lost her breath when her gaze landed on yet another person in the room—one in a wheelchair. Coach Wade Landon.

"You should call Sheriff Norwood."

Reyna recognized the voice of the man who had spoken. Not the coach or the priest…or Ward. Her head swiveled around, sending her attention beyond where the Widows sat, and then she spotted Gordon Walls. She started in his direction, stalling just shy of reaching him. He was handcuffed to a chair.

She stared back at Birdie. "What is going on here? Why is he in handcuffs?"

The fact that he'd had a motive to get rid of at least one of the Three wasn't lost on Reyna. For that matter, it seemed everyone in the room had a motive.

"Please, Reyna," Birdie said. "We've been waiting for your time to arrive. Your seat is at the desk. You'll find the pens and pencils and the notepad you need to assist in what we have to do."

"What is it you have to do?" She had a very bad feeling about where this was going.

"We're conducting a trial," Birdie explained. "We need you to be our official recorder."

"Stenographer," Eudora corrected.

Frustration pumped through Reyna. "Eudora, the center believes you've been kidnapped. They have called in the authorities."

She made a face that said *so what?* "That place needed a little excitement."

Reyna wheeled on Birdie. "How did you get her out?"

Birdie shrugged. "I used yesterday's pass. No one seemed to notice, and they didn't make me sign in since I had one."

Reyna's jaw dropped. "That's why you called me to your bedside yesterday. You weren't ailing more than usual. You just needed Birdie to get a visitor's pass."

Eudora smiled patiently. "We do what we must."

Okay. Reyna was sure now. These people—every single one of them, except maybe Deputy Walls—was on something. Alcohol, drugs…something.

"Reyna," the priest said, "humor us. Take your seat and prepare to take notes. You don't have to record everything verbatim, just the important parts."

No way. She moved her head side to side. "I'm not doing anything until you tell me what's going on here." Her attention landed on Ward. "Your grandson is frantic to find you. What in the world are you doing?"

"Sit down, Reyna," he said in the voice that she imagined he had used to scold his son and his grandson when necessary. "You'll know what you need to very shortly."

If his gaze hadn't held hers so steadily…so urgently… she would have walked out and promptly called the sheriff. He needed her to do this. She looked from one person to the next. They all needed her to cooperate. Whatever their reasons, how could she say no?

She turned lastly to Eudora, who gave her a reassuring and somehow hopeful look.

"If I'm staying," Reyna countered, "you have to let me call Ben. He should be here."

Heads started to shake. When Reyna would have argued, Ward spoke up again. "His being here would make him culpable. We can't allow that."

"But I can be culpable?" she asked, mostly to buy time to think of another reason to call Ben.

"We brought you here under false pretense," Birdie explained. "You are not here of your own volition."

There was no point arguing with these people. "Okay." She walked to the desk and sat down, grabbed a pen and readied the notepad. Besides, Ben would come back looking for her.

Birdie suggested, "You might want to list all those present, yourself included." She stepped forward and addressed the group. "Ward, Eudora." She shifted her attention to the Widows. "Lucinda, Deidre, Harlowe. The five of you are the jury."

For the love of God. They really were having a trial. Reyna looked from the coach to the priest and then to Walls. But who was the defendant?

"Deputy Walls, you are a special witness."

"Ms. Birdie," he shot back, "if you take these cuffs off now, I won't tell a soul about you luring me here with that story about a break-in and then feeding me those brownies that put me out for—"

"Order in the courtroom," Father Cullen demanded.

His harsh tone yanked Reyna's attention in his direction.

Noting her focus on the man, Birdie said, "Father Cullen is our judge."

So it was Coach Landon. Reyna's gaze landed on him

next. He stared back, fear in his eyes, sweat beading on his forehead.

Walls was right—they needed to call the sheriff. She reached into her bag for her cell. It was suddenly yanked from her reach.

Reyna glared at Birdie. "What are you doing?"

Birdie glared right back. "We all gathered here late yesterday to determine how best to move forward. The decision was unanimous. It took some doing to get prepared to proceed but we're ready now. There is no going back, Reyna. Believe that if you believe nothing else. We have run out of time."

Reyna surveyed those present. Her gaze settled on Ben's mother. "He's worried sick about you."

"You'll understand soon," Lucinda assured her. "We've all seen to our final arrangements and we are now doing what we have to do."

Horror pounded Reyna in the chest. Was this going to be some sort of mass suicide?

"We're wasting time," Cullen announced. "We should begin and we will conduct ourselves appropriately as we proceed." He looked directly at Reyna. "And no one is leaving until this is done."

"Thirty years ago," Birdie began but hesitated. She turned to Reyna. "I'm sorry—I forgot to tell you that I'm the prosecutor."

Reyna drew in a deep breath and looked around the room. Okay, if this was the way it was going to be, there was one thing missing. "He needs an attorney."

Birdie flashed her a look of annoyance. "He waived the right to an attorney." She pointed her attention at Coach Landon. "Isn't that right, Landon?"

He nodded, his eyes wide and bulging with unadulterated fear.

Birdie smiled at Reyna. "There you go."

"Thirty years ago," she said again before Reyna could protest more, "Ward Kane Junior, Duke Fuller and Judson Evans disappeared, and as far as the authorities are concerned, their case remains unsolved." She looked from one of those present to the next. "But we all know differently."

Heads nodded, and agreements rumbled through those gathered.

"You're all going to be arrested," Walls warned.

"Shut up, Gordon," Ward snapped.

Reyna opted not to write that down. All she could hope to do was be patient and be ready to stop any harm from happening.

"Coach Landon," Birdie said, "can you tell us about your relationship with the three missing men who came to be known as the Three?"

He heaved out a breath. "Everyone here knows I was their coach from middle school through high school."

"When would you say the trouble began between you and these men?" Birdie asked.

Landon shrugged. "At that ten-year reunion. Duke got jealous—"

"Liar!"

Reyna jumped at the word Deidre Fuller had hurled at the man.

"Tell them when it began," she roared like a mama bear protecting its cub.

"Let me remind you," the priest said to Landon, "I know the whole truth. I will know if you lie."

Reyna stared at the man of God, the keeper of the secrets. Dear God, it was him. He knew the truth. Why had he never told anyone? Had any of the Widows told him within the sanctity of the vow of confession? Was this his way of helping see that justice was finally done? He was dying—Father Jordan had said as much.

Understanding settled on Reyna like a load of bricks. He was dying, and he wanted to make this right before he died. Her gaze swung to Ward Kane. He figured his days were numbered as well… He wanted the truth. Her gaze swept across the room. They all wanted something more than just the truth… They wanted justice.

Landon shook his head frantically. "I can't. I can't talk about it."

"Deputy Walls." Birdie turned toward the man handcuffed to his chair. "We'd like you to tell us the relevant events you saw and heard the day the Three went missing."

The deputy glared at Birdie, shook his head. "I was at the diner. I overheard a tense conversation where JR told Duke 'it was the only way.' Duke didn't seem to agree, but Judson was ready to go with whatever plan JR had."

"Did they mention where they were going?" Birdie asked.

He stared at the floor for a moment.

"Answer the question," Cullen demanded.

"They were meeting Coach Landon to confront him."

Reyna's breath exited her lungs so sharply it hurt. "Have you known this all along?" she demanded.

"You don't get to ask questions," Cullen warned.

Reyna stood. "This has gone far enough," she snapped. She walked toward Walls. "You knew they were meeting with Coach Landon, and you never told anyone." It wasn't a question. His own words had just confirmed as much because she hadn't found a single statement he'd given thirty years ago that said where the Three had been going the day they had disappeared.

"He had his reasons," Birdie said, "but we're correcting that slip now. It's going on the record." She nodded to Reyna. "Write it down."

Reluctantly, Reyna went back to the desk and wrote the statement on the notepad hard enough to indent every page beneath it.

"You were saying," Birdie said, her voice hard.

Walls said nothing.

"Finish your statement," Cullen ordered, "or I will answer it for you."

Walls sneered at him. "You can't. You took a vow."

Cullen laughed, a dry sound. "What do I care about what man can do to me? My fate will lie with the Heavenly Father, and I'm good with whatever He decides."

"I knew why they wanted to confront him," Walls admitted reluctantly. "I knew it was the reason Duke went off at the reunion when the scumbag talked about little Jesse Carson."

"Will you please identify the scumbag you mean?" Birdie directed.

"Landon." He looked anywhere but at the man in the wheelchair.

"He's lying," Landon cried. "He killed them to get back at Lucinda for choosing someone else besides him."

"This," Walls roared, "was never about Lucinda. It was about Landon and the monster he kept hidden all those years."

"We know what you did," Lucinda charged.

"We're no longer satisfied with what you've lost," Harlowe snarled. "We want you to pay the price you should have all those years ago, even if we have to pay for the mistake we made trusting you."

"We should have known you wouldn't stand by your word," Deidre said with utter disdain. "You're a coward."

"You can't prove any of it," Landon argued. "You never had any evidence, and you never will." He laughed. "Have your fun. The worst you can do is try finishing what you started thirty years ago." He swung his attention to Reyna.

She flinched at his ugly stare.

"Are you going to be a witness to them killing me, or are you going to save me?" he asked. "The way I see it, you're the only chance I've got of surviving this."

All eyes rested on Reyna then. Heart pounding, she moistened her lips and said the only thing she could think to say. "Tell me what you did, and I'll tell you what I can do." Sounded fair enough. She was here for answers, after all. At the moment she just needed to buy time. Ben would be coming back at some point. She prayed it was sooner rather than later.

"You had a choice, Landon," Cullen said, drawing the room's attention back to him. "You made the wrong one."

Landon shot him a look. "I think I'll just wait until you're in hell. I hear you're headed that way real soon."

The jury started shouting again.

"Order!" When the shouting continued, Cullen stood. "I said shut up and listen! We're likely short on time here." He glanced at Reyna. "Ben will probably show up anytime. We can't be sure how long he and Sheriff Norwood will be distracted."

Reyna felt her jaw drop again. These people had set this up—all of it.

The arguing and shouting ceased instantly.

"When we found out what he'd done," Deidre said, clearly speaking to Reyna, "we gave him a choice."

"Deidre," Cullen warned.

"If we expect her cooperation," she argued, "we need to explain. Otherwise we will run out of time."

"Just get this over with," Walls whined. "Kidnapping is a serious crime."

Reyna looked from one to the next. She had so many questions, but she didn't want to stop their conversation, afraid it would disrupt the truth from coming out.

Lucinda stood next to Deidre. She pointed to Landon. "He chose Duke Fuller when he was just ten years old."

Deidre wilted back onto the sofa and put her face in her hands.

"For the next six years," Lucinda went on, "he used Duke to make videos, which he sold to the highest bidder. When Duke tried to make him stop, Landon threatened to tell his friends and his parents. To take him off the team."

Deidre was crying now.

Reyna felt sick. Harlowe hugged her friend close and swiped at her own tears. Eudora and Birdie held each other, and they cried too.

"Walls," Cullen said, "do you have anything to say?"

He glared at Cullen. "He did the same thing to me."

"Why didn't you tell anyone?" Reyna demanded.

Cullen lifted his eyebrows at her, but she ignored him.

"Why?" she demanded.

"Who was going to believe me over the town's beloved coach?" Walls snarled. "Even now, the school is planning to give him a lifetime achievement award. He hasn't coached in nearly thirty years, and still his coaching record rises above all else."

Ward stood. "That is our fault," he snapped. "If we'd

told the world the truth when we discovered it, everyone would have known and the bastard would be rotting in prison now. Instead, we did what we thought was right to protect the reputation of the boys."

"No," Cullen said. "He wouldn't be in prison. We had no real evidence. And even if we had been able to convince anyone, the most he would have gotten was ten years."

"For murder?" Ward howled.

The anguish in his words ripped at Reyna's heart.

"You know we couldn't prove the murders," Cullen argued. "The best we could have hoped for was child pornography. He never touched the boys, as far as we know—it was only the videos."

Reyna stood again. "You all believe that Coach Landon killed those men?"

"We know he did," Ward said. "We just can't prove it."

"He was seen coming from the funeral home that night," Walls said. "The night they disappeared."

"We believe," Harlowe said, "that he drugged them or poisoned them when they went to confront him and then cremated their bodies. He worked summers and on occasions throughout the year at Addison Funeral Home. That's why we never found them." She dropped back to the sofa, and the Widows held each other and struggled with their composure.

Reyna's heart was in her throat. "How do you know they went to confront him?"

If these women knew all this thirty years ago, why the hell hadn't they told someone?

"They didn't know until I told them," Cullen said. "After the incident at the reunion, Duke came to me and told me everything. He said he'd finally told his best friends, and they had insisted on going with him to confront Landon. He asked me to pray for them, and he gave me his cross to pray over until it was finished."

"Why the hell didn't you tell anyone?" Reyna demanded. The explanation certainly clarified why the cross was in the rectory. But it didn't explain what her FBI friend had told her. "Were you afraid the police would connect you to your own secret?"

All eyes were on Reyna again.

Cullen's gaze remained locked with hers as he answered the accusation. "My secret is only that I witnessed something I could not unsee. For that, my former life had to be left behind. And that, Ms. Hart, is for another time. Not today."

He was in witness protection. She nodded. "You're right. Forgive me."

"They're going to kill me," Landon cried. "They already tried once. You can't let them do this."

"Shut up, you bastard," Walls snarled. "You should have died in that fire, and maybe the rest of us would have had some peace the last three decades." He jerked at his restraints. "Take off these cuffs," he commanded, "and I'll end this now."

"And here you thought," Cullen said, "we secured you to keep you from escaping."

Walls glared at him. "This is not going to end the way you hope." He shifted his glower to Reyna. "Not now."

"Tell the truth, Landon," Eudora said, standing with the help of Birdie, "and this will be over. You can be arrested, and we can go on with what's left of our lives."

Landon shook his head. "You have no evidence, and I'm not saying anything." He swung his attention to Reyna. "They tried to kill me—are you aware of that? This so-called priest got me drunk and left me passed out on the floor of my bedroom. Then he left, and they—" he pointed to the Widows "—set my house on fire. It's a miracle I woke up and was able to jump out the window." He glared at the women. "You're lucky I never said a word. I kept your secret."

Ward jabbed a finger in the man's direction. "You murdered my son and his friends. Nothing you have suffered mitigates murder."

"Prove it," Landon challenged.

Reyna surveyed the crowd… No one said a word.

Because they didn't have the one thing they needed… *proof.*

Chapter Fifteen

Whispering Winds High School
School Road
4:30 p.m.

“Telling you not to worry is pointless,” Norwood said, “so I won’t bother. But I can tell you that we will find your grandfather.”

Ben shrugged. “Yeah, well, that’s what they told my mother and my grandfather all those years ago about my father.”

“I guess I deserved that one.” Norwood stared at the ground a moment. “There’s something going on, Ben. Something that your grandfather and the Widows are twisted up in. I don’t know what exactly, but truth is it’s got me worried.” She eyed him skeptically. “You don’t know what that might be, do you?”

Ben considered the idea that he probably shouldn’t go on the record about anything, but he knew Tara Norwood and, more importantly, he trusted her. “Eudora Davenport contracted Reyna to come here and dig around in the disappearance. My grandfather agreed to be a part of it. My mom and Harlowe Evans talked to her, but Deidre Fuller refused. We’ve met with Father Cullen, Coach Landon and anyone else who would talk to her or to us both.”

"All these strange things started to happen after Reyna came to town, right?"

"This is not her doing," Ben argued. "I'm not sharing this information with you to have you thinking Reyna is responsible for any of this, because that's not true at all. She has no idea who is behind all this. I think whoever it is, they're using her to…" He shrugged. "I don't know, call attention to the story, something."

"Obviously the retired priest didn't tell you anything."

Ben thought of the cross they'd found in his room. He decided it was best for now if he kept that to himself. "He did not."

"Have you learned anything," she asked, "that wasn't already a part of discovery in the original investigation?"

For a moment—a single moment—he considered again telling her all he knew. About the cross, the new suspicions he had about Coach Landon given the incident at the high school reunion. But he kicked the idea away.

"I can't say that we've learned anything you can grab on to and say here, this makes a difference. But there are pieces missing, and I think there are folks who have those pieces who haven't come forward."

She nodded. "So that's a yes."

He wasn't really surprised she understood he was being evasive. She was the sheriff. "Nothing I feel confident in sharing."

"You let me know if you change your mind. Meanwhile, I'll call you if we find anything or hear from anyone who's seen Ward."

"Thanks. I appreciate all you're doing, Sheriff Norwood."

"You just remember you said that if you find something you believe I need to know."

Now he felt guilty for not coming clean. "Yes, ma'am."

"One more thing," she said before letting him go. "That little cabin over on Trout Lake."

Maybe she'd been holding something back too. "Did you find anything?"

"Not really, but there was something odd about it." She set her hands on her hips and pinched her lips together for a moment. "The wood it was built from was old, but we determined that it had been put together out there just recently. There was no dust, no cobwebs, nothing to suggest it had been there long at all. We're thinking someone put it there, like, last week. Oddly enough, we found several items hidden behind photos and the jerseys that pointed to Wade Landon as having been the one who set the place up. There were notes in his handwriting about games and players. The sort of thing someone like him would keep in school files. There were Polaroid-type snapshots of him with the Three going back to their peewee football days. Just random stuff that appeared to have come from Landon. In fact, I sent a deputy to the school and checked on any files he might have had. All his files had been retired, as expected, but when the deputy and the administrator went to pull those files, they were missing. Any thoughts on how a man in a wheelchair could have made that happen?"

"Not offhand." He wasn't about to tell her that he had a sneaking suspicion his grandfather and maybe his mother and the other Widows might've been involved. Wow. How had they managed that—assuming they had—without him knowing?

Norwood nodded. "If you figure it out, you let me know."

"Yes, ma'am." Sounded like she'd already figured it out.

Ben headed back to his truck. Norwood had said that he could pick up his grandfather's truck when they'd finished processing it.

As he drove away, he deliberated on the idea of paying another visit to Landon. He and Reyna had talked about interviewing him again. Considering what he'd just learned from Norwood, a quick stop at the man's place wouldn't take long. Then he'd join Reyna at the Jewel. He figured everything must have been okay since she hadn't called to say otherwise.

The one thing on his mind right now was that if his grandfather and the Widows thought Landon had something to do with the disappearance, then he'd be a fool not to lean in that same direction.

Landon Residence
Harding Drive
5:30 p.m.

BEN WAS JUST about to knock on the door when he noticed that it was ajar. "Coach Landon!"

The house was silent inside. He glanced around the yard, up and down the street. No pedestrians. No vehicles coming or going.

Ben pushed the door open and stepped inside. "Mr. Landon? You home?"

No response.

He surveyed the living room. No sign of a struggle or any sort of foul play. Nothing out of place based on his one other visit here. He moved on to the kitchen. He opened the back door and checked the small yard that was more of a fenced-in patio-sized patch of grass. The gate on the back side of the fence was partially open. Four long strides later and he looked beyond the gate to find an alley. No cars, no one passing through on foot. He closed the gate and went back into the cottage. The place was small. Only one story and less than a thousand square feet. It took only a few seconds to poke his head through the doors of the two bedrooms and the one bathroom.

No Coach Landon. Like the rest of the place, the bedrooms showed no indication there had been trouble.

It was possible Landon had been picked up for a trip to the market. But why leave his front door ajar?

Ben knew he should call the sheriff...but first he needed a look. As illegal as it was, this might be his only chance.

He walked through the place again, more slowly this time. The second bedroom was a sort of office with a desk and computer. He touched the mouse and awakened the screen, which requested a passcode. A quick look through the drawers of the desk revealed only the usual—personal files, medical, insurance, tax returns. The closet was basically empty—a couple of heavy winter coats and a vacuum cleaner.

The bathroom fixtures, like everything else in the house, were handicap accessible. Beyond the prescription bottles of painkillers, there was little else of interest in the bathroom.

Moving on, he went back into the guy's bedroom. Though he should have felt guilty going through his stuff, he didn't. Ben had already crossed a line there was no going back from. He needed answers, and that was driving him.

His grandfather and his mother were missing. He was beyond reason at this point.

The latest information Norwood had passed along only made him more certain he and Reyna were getting close to the truth.

After picking through all the drawers and under the bed, he came up empty-handed. The only place left to look was the closet. Two rows of shirts more suited to twenty or thirty years ago hung one over the other. A handle enabled the top row to be pulled down to the same level as the lower rack.

On the wall behind the hanging shirts on the lower rack was something blue. Ben parted the shirts and found himself staring at a school football jersey. He considered that maybe it was the coach's, but then the number exploded in his brain.

18

Duke Fuller's number.

Ben reached out, took the jersey by the hanger and removed it from the clip where it hung. It was a little different from the one hanging in the cabin. Smaller, he decided. Maybe from sophomore or junior year. A small door—rustic and obviously homemade—on the wall, down closer to the floor behind where the jersey had hung, caught his eye. Ben crouched down and opened the door. Behind it was a niche built into the wall. Every square inch was covered with photos and newspaper clippings about the Three. Was this another shrine to the missing men? He doubted Landon could have built the one at Trout Lake in his condition. But this he could do. Or he could have hired someone to build it, for that matter.

Along the bottom of the built-in was a small wooden box shaped like the typical treasure chest. He opened it, and inside were three small velvet pull-string bags—the kind jewelers used. He tugged one open. It held dust or…

The air stalled in his lungs. *Ash.*

"Holy…"

His brain told him not to do it, but he wasn't operating with his brain right now. He grabbed the bags and hurried back to the front door. He had to get to Reyna…

If he was right…he'd found the Three.

The Jewel Bed & Breakfast
Main Street
6:15 p.m.

BEN SKIDDED TO a stop in the parking area. He considered again that he should have called Sheriff Norwood. He glanced at the velvet bags on the passenger seat. There was this thing called chain of custody. He'd already screwed that up, but he hadn't been able to leave the bags behind. If Coach Landon returned home before Ben could do whatever the hell it was he intended to do with this… He couldn't let that happen.

He reached behind to the back floorboard and grabbed the plastic bag from the hardware store that held those three-inch wood screws he'd picked up days ago for the Henry project. He dumped the screws and tucked the velvet bags inside. Bag in hand, he climbed out of the truck and rushed to the front entrance of the Jewel. Locked.

Dang it! He banged on the door. "Ms. Birdie! Reyna!"

He waited. No one came to the door. She had to be here. He'd left her here. If she'd had reason to go somewhere else, she would have called him. He checked his cell just in case he'd missed a call or text message. Nothing.

"Where are you?" He tapped her name in his contacts and waited for the phone to ring. No answer after the first ring. Another ring…

He drew the phone away from his ear and listened.

He could still hear the ringing…not from his phone but from somewhere beyond the front door.

Another bang on the door. "Reyna!"

If something had happened to her…

Still no answer.

"If you don't allow me to let him in," Reyna argued, "he'll go to the sheriff." She glowered at Ward. "He's already worried sick about you." She glanced at Lucinda then. "And you."

Ward held her gaze for a moment, then said, "Let him be a part of this."

Reyna didn't wait for the responses of the others. She stepped around Birdie and hurried along the seemingly endless hall until she reached the door. She flipped the dead bolt and swung the door open. Ben had started down the steps.

"Ben."

He turned around.

She looked at the street beyond him, then motioned for him to come inside. Worry etched across his face, he joined her at the door.

"How's Birdie?" He searched her eyes, probably saw the confusion and worry there.

"Come with me." She grabbed him by the hand and ushered him inside. She closed and locked the door.

Holding on to his hand, she started down that long hall.

"Where are we going?"

Just before reaching the doors, she paused, turned to him. "I need you to brace yourself. Don't get angry or…" She shrugged. "Just stay calm and listen."

He nodded. "I'll do my best."

She opened the pocket doors and led him into the parlor where the others waited.

"Pops." His full attention settled on his grandfather. "Sheriff Norwood is looking for you. We've got folks all over town keeping an eye out for you."

"I'm sorry," Ward said. "I had to keep you in the dark, but it was necessary."

"We had no choice," his mother said, her voice and expression urging him to understand.

What the hell was going on here?

Ben scanned the room, noting the faces there. Confusion furrowed his brow, and he turned to Reyna. "Is Walls handcuffed to that chair?"

She nodded. "I'm afraid so."

"What the hell is going on here?" he demanded of no one in particular, all signs of uncertainty gone from his voice now.

"We need to proceed," Father Cullen said. "We're too close to let this opportunity be spoiled by the arrival of the sheriff's department."

Ben looked to Reyna again. "What's he talking about?"

"There is no time," Ward said. "We will catch you up when this is done."

"Mr. Landon," Cullen said, "we have motive, means, and we have opportunity. You had reason to want the Three to disappear. I am witness to that. Duke Fuller told me himself that he, Judson Evans and JR Kane would be meeting with you that evening." Cullen looked in Ben's direction. "The evening the Three left their homes for the last time and never returned." He turned back to Landon then. "There is an eyewitness who saw you leaving the funeral home, where you had access to a crematorium, late that night. Your employer at the funeral home stated that you had your own key but insisted that no one was working that night."

Landon shook his head. "You're wasting your time. You can talk about how I had motive and whatever else you want to drum up—you can keep spinning your fairy tales about how you think I did this or that. But none of it matters because you have no evidence."

The realization of what they were talking about slammed into Ben. He held up a hardware-store bag. Reyna looked from the bag to him and likely tried to imagine what was inside and how it could be important.

"You mean this?" he asked, his attention fixed on the coach.

Landon turned to Ben. He shook his head. "I have no idea what you have in that bag."

Ben reached into the bag and pulled out another smaller one. Black. With a gold string that pulled together to tighten the opening.

"There are three of these small sacks," Ben explained. "They were hidden in the little shrine you created in your closet, Coach Landon. I'm guessing what's inside are cremated remains—ashes." He shrugged. "Not all of them, obviously, but a portion. Maybe enough to keep close by, to remind you of what you'd done."

Landon's face paled, his jaw fell slack, but not a word came out of his mouth.

7:00 p.m.

BEFORE THE REAL fray started, Reyna called the center and reported that Eudora had been found and was safe. Reyna would get her back there in the morning.

Minutes later Sheriff Norwood and two of her deputies arrived, and that was when the frenzy exploded. Crime scene investigators were called. Paramedics were next, since Landon appeared to be on the verge of a heart attack. Walls had been uncuffed before Norwood had arrived. So far he hadn't told the sheriff that Ward Kane had kidnapped him. All involved had come of their own free will, except Walls and Landon. Both of whom Birdie and Ward had basically abducted.

Everyone involved, except Reyna and Ben, had been lined up in chairs in the long hall. A deputy stood guard, ensuring they didn't talk among themselves.

Norwood and the other deputy were interviewing the group one at a time. They had already interviewed Reyna and Ben, which was why they weren't seated in that line.

Once the other interviews were underway, Reyna had taken Ben to the kitchen and conveyed all that she had heard and seen before he'd arrived.

"You're saying Father Cullen had nothing to do with what happened. Duke gave him the cross and chain."

Reyna nodded. "That's correct."

"What about the other thing your FBI friend mentioned?"

"Cullen is in witness protection." Reyna shrugged. "He will report to his point of contact when this is done. Considering his health and if no one involved spills his secret, he may be able to stay here."

Ben braced his hands on either side of him on the kitchen counter. He'd been leaning there since she'd started talking. She understood completely. The entire story was difficult to believe… It was the sort of thing mystery movies were made of.

But it was true… It was real life.

Ben's life and the lives of all the other people lined up in that long hall.

Reyna had a feeling this was going to be a long night.

Chapter Sixteen

Kane Residence
Lula Lake Lane
Saturday, April 27, 2:20 p.m.

Eudora had decided not to return to the center. Birdie intended to temporarily close the Jewel so that she could take care of the woman she loved with all her heart until her time on this earth was done.

Reyna felt confident this was the right decision. Hospice would help when the time came. Until then, the two could enjoy Eudora's every lucid moment.

Reyna had packed her few things, only then realizing that she still had some of Birdie's clothes. She'd have to drop them off.

Reyna zipped the borrowed bag. She'd have to drop that off too. She laughed, looked around the room. She'd only slept in this room one night. She'd spent the rest of her time with Ben…in his room.

It wasn't going to be easy to go back to her life since he wasn't in it. But she couldn't put off going back forever.

"No use beating around the bush."

She walked out of the room and headed down the stairs. It was time to leave.

The whole story was out in the open now. No more secrets about the missing Three or the Widows. The players, the good ones and the bad ones, had been revealed.

Lucinda had explained that the note and the tire damage had been pulled off by the Widows. They hadn't meant for Reyna to be hurt—the tire thing hadn't turned out the way they'd expected. Birdie had started the fire in Reyna's room at the bed-and-breakfast. All was a ruse designed to support the idea that Reyna might be getting close to the truth. Eudora had told them that Reyna was smart, so they had to be prepared to draw her deeper into the mystery. To keep her motivated to find the pieces of the puzzle. The disappearance of Ward and the Widows had been an attempt to keep Ben and Sheriff Norwood distracted. All had known Ben would start to worry if his grandfather and mother suddenly weren't around for the length of time expected to do what needed to be done leading up to the mock trial.

The failing health of Ward and the priest had prompted the two to consider whether they wanted to leave this earth without finding a way for the truth to be revealed. But when they had learned about the lifetime achievement award that Landon would receive, the gloves had come off and they had made a pact to do whatever necessary to see that justice was done before that happened.

The Widows had been brought in on the plan first. Together, they and Ward had erected that cabin shrine to point to Landon. As for Eudora and Birdie, they were the witnesses who'd seen Landon leaving the funeral home that night. Later they'd realized he had likely been up to no good, but they'd had no proof and the man had worked at the funeral home part-time. Still, they had brought their concerns to their priest, and that was how they had become a part of the group.

This group of savvy seniors had even planned for what came after their journey to deliver justice. Father Cullen had taken complete responsibility for the fire at the Landon home thirty years ago. He'd explained that the two of them, he and Landon, had been drinking and smoking cigars. At some point in the evening Landon had started to cry and asked if Cullen could perform the sacrament of confession, during which he admitted to pushing his wife down the stairs because she'd found out about his secret obsession. Since Landon had told Cullen this in confidence, he hadn't been able to bring it to the police. At least, until now. Now he was prepared to break his vows for the greater good.

Deputy Gordon Walls had given a statement as to what he'd overheard the Three discussing about confronting Landon on the day they'd disappeared. He said nothing of having been kidnapped and brought to the meeting at the Jewel. Birdie and Eudora gave their own statements about what they had witnessed that long-ago night when they saw Landon coming out of the funeral home.

With Ben's find of the ashes in the man's home, Landon had decided to confess. He'd blurted his confession before Sheriff Norwood could mention that there would likely be legal challenges regarding the find in his home. Considering he'd admitted to murdering the Three and cremating their bodies as well as pushing his wife to her death, Landon was going away for a very, very long time.

It was going to make an amazing story, and the whole group wanted Reyna to write it. She hoped she could do their incredible tale justice.

Downstairs, Ward, Ben and Lucinda waited for her. Her chest tightened at the idea of leaving.

Ward hugged her first. "Thank you, Reyna, for helping us get this done."

"Well, I don't know how much help I was, but I suppose my being here did move things along a bit."

Lucinda stepped forward and hugged her next. "Thank you." She drew back and glanced at her son. "For helping me give my son his father back. We're having a memorial week after next. I hope you'll come."

Reyna smiled, her lips quivering a little. "I wouldn't miss it for the world."

Ward cleared his throat. "Lucinda and I should check things out at the barn."

Ben's mother nodded. "That's right. We'll be a few minutes."

Ben laughed as the two left the room. "I have no idea what's in the barn that those two need to check, but I think that was code for giving us some privacy."

Reyna couldn't hold back her own smile. She was immensely grateful that his family was finally whole again. His father was still gone, but at least they had each other now with no more secrets between them. "I think you are probably right." She took a breath. "So I guess this is goodbye."

"Guess so."

"You walking me to my car?"

"Absolutely." He reached for her bag. "I'll take that."

He opened the door and followed her out onto the porch. It was such a nice day. The air was clean and crisp. Whispering Winds really was a nice town.

They descended the steps together and walked to her Land Rover. He stowed the bag in the back seat and joined her at the driver's-side door.

"I hope I see you again," he said, his eyes searching hers.

"We could make a date," she suggested. "Have dinner in the city."

He nodded. "Works for me."

Then he hugged her hard. She hugged him right back just as firmly. She never wanted to let go.

He drew back just far enough to kiss her gently on the lips. "I'm going to miss you, Reyna Hart."

"I'll miss you too."

Reyna blinked at the emotion burning her eyes as she climbed into her Land Rover. It wasn't like she wasn't going to see him again or that she was that far away, but her emotions apparently had a mind of their own.

He closed her door, and she started the engine. With one last wave, she backed up, pointed the vehicle toward town and drove away from him.

It had been a really long time since her heart had hurt so much. She wasn't sure if she could bear it. She had just reached the end of the long drive when she hit her brakes. She stared into the rearview mirror. He was still standing there watching her.

"No way am I driving away from this guy."

She shifted into Reverse, turned around and drove back up to the house. She shoved the gearshift into Park, opened the door and climbed out.

"Did you forget something?" he asked, looking confused and maybe a little hopeful.

She reached for the back door to retrieve her borrowed bag. "No. I just decided that if I'm going to do this story justice, I need to be here, in the setting." She paused and looked to him. "You okay with me staying with you for the next few months?"

A grin slid across his face. "I'm more than okay with

it." He grabbed her and kissed her on the lips. "Be careful, Ms. Hart—I might not ever let you get away."

She was more than okay with that.

* * * * *